The Eyes

of Love

J.E. Smythe

WRITE**LEG**
PUBLISHING, LLC

The Eyes of Love

Copyright © 2019 J.E. Smythe

Write LEG books may be ordered through booksellers or by Contacting

Write LEG Publishing
P.O. Box 790672
Charlotte, North Carolina 28206
www.writeleg.com

Editing by Erica L. James
Cover Design by Lynda Payton

Soft Cover: ISBN 978-0-9979175-4-3
E-book: ISBN 978-0-9979175-5-0
Audiobook: ISBN 978-0-9979175-6-7

Table of Contents

Part 1:

In the Beginning

J.E. Smythe

Ruth

Often, we look at love as this nonexistent thing. A mirage that will never come to pass. As if there are those that are meant to walk down the aisle and have their happily ever after and then there's the rest of us: the chronically single, always alone but never lonely, at least not outwardly so, women who hold on to their dignity with one hand and waive away the "what's wrong with her" stares with the other hand.

It's those stares that constantly remind us that no matter what we do it will never be enough because we lack one very important thing, love.

It's the one thing that escapes us the one imperfection. As if some souls were meant to connect and others were meant to roam this earth all on their own. If the stories of love are correct, then the souls that are meant to find one another will eventually find one another like some cosmic collision. There's no way around it; it has to happen, as if the earth will not be complete until these two souls are brought together.

So then what about the rest of us? Perhaps the world will be just fine if we're left out on our own. Maybe not all souls are meant to collide with another, at least that's what I tell myself. It sometimes helps but then as always, I tend to ask follow up questions like: who decides? Or what the hell is so wrong with me that I didn't make the cut? Then there are the questions that haunt me daily: what if the soul that I was supposed to connect with already came and I was so busy doing other things that it just moved on to someone else?

"Who the hell says that women have to be barefoot and pregnant to prove that they're women enough?" Mona shouted out.

Mona Jackson and I met in college and we hit it off right away. She was the self-proclaimed independent, "I don't need a man for anything" type of woman. She owned her own art gallery in uptown Charlotte, NC and lived in the loft apartment right above the gallery. Mona loved her living conditions; she was never too far from a party and she loved to party. Mona was like the wingman, the one who gets in your ear to do things that you would never do on your own.

"It's not about being barefoot and pregnant," Gloria replied. "It's about finding your partner, the one person that has your back."

I met Gloria Daniels in college also. She and Mona were cousins and the total opposite of one another. Gloria married her high school sweetheart right out of college and they lived in the suburbs in a big single family house with their two beautiful daughters. Far away from the hustle and bustle of Uptown living. Gloria was that angel over your shoulder who warned you to stay away from the Monas of the world.

Gloria loved love and wanted all her friends to experience what true love felt like. So, she never wasted a moment to remind us to never give up on finding that special person.

"Girl bye," Mona chuckled. "There's a

whole lotta divorced women out here whose husbands ran around, cheated and embarrassed the hell outa them that will disagree with you right now."

"Okay, hold on," I interrupted. "I'm not saying that love is this four letter word. . ."

"Hell, I am," Mona added as she took a drink of her wine.

I shot her a dirty look and then continued. "All I'm saying is, there's nothing wrong with either choosing to not be married or choosing not to settle for less just to say you're married."

"I get it, Ruth, and I'm not saying there's anything wrong with you. I just know that you have passed up on some pretty great guys all because they don't fit on some list," Gloria said.

"It's not about fitting on some list. If I've worked hard and sacrificed so much, why do I have to sacrifice with the type of guy that I want? Why can't I ask for what I feel I deserve in a man? We all can't be lucky enough to find Prince Charming straight out of high school, Gloria," I replied.

"Preach girl, you better preach!" Mona shouted out with her head tilted back and her two hands waiving in the air.

"Just because you didn't find your Prince Charming in high school doesn't mean he's not out there," Gloria replied.

"Girrrrrrrrrrrllll," Mona sighed. "If you met your man right out of high school, how you know he's the right one if you ain't had none other? You know what I'm saying. I mean, there's so many tasty treats out there; how you know your treat is the best of the bunch?"

I let out a loud burst of laughter as

Gloria stared at Mona with frustration. The differences between Mona and Gloria amused me, and I couldn't help but think that it amused the two of them as well.

"You know what, I'm about to go home to my kids and husband," Gloria replied.

"Oh yes, and I'm about to go home to my vibrator," Mona replied. "There's no arguing or fussing. Nobody cares who took out the trash or who paid what bill. We just get right to it and it's absolutely lovely."

"Really? A vibrator? That's supposed to take the place of a good man?" Gloria asked.

"You obviously haven't had the right vibrator in your life. I'm talking about the fully charged, full throttle one. Don't worry girl; I'll get you one for your birthday," Mona smirked.

"Nope, I'm good. Thank you," Gloria

said as she walked toward the door.

"You sure girl because I get a discount?" Mona said as she followed behind.

"You know what, I'll talk to you guys later," I said as I opened the front door.

"Good night, Ruth. I'll call you tomorrow," Gloria said.

"Alright girl, I'll see you when I see you. I'm about to hit the club," Mona said.

"What? It's like 11:30 at night," Gloria said turning to look at Mona disapprovingly.

"Girl, and? Nobody goes to the club before twelve. See, single women know that," Mona said.

"You know, I'm going. It's enough for tonight, Mona," Gloria said as she walked away.

"Bye," I giggled as I closed the door

behind them.

My house grew still and quiet after my friends left as I began to reflect on our conversation. I started to clean up the glasses left on the coffee table. But as I stood in the kitchen, I heard the captivating sound of a saxophone playing in the distance. I had grown accustomed to the sound for the past few weeks, ever since my new neighbor moved into the house on the other side of my fence.

I hadn't seen or met this new neighbor, but I was happy for the momentary noise that broke through the quietness of my surroundings.

I grabbed the bottle of wine and a blanket and walked out onto my back porch. I sat on my swing chair and covered myself with the blanket. The warm Charlotte air ran across my face as I took a sip of wine from the bottle and laid my head back on the swing chair and allowed the saxophone to serenade me.

When you're single, your relationship status becomes everyone's business. But when you're single after a particular age, it becomes everyone's mission to find you just the right guy, or at least who they deem to be the right guy. It's a constant reminder that you have failed tragically at life and now everyone else has to fix it.

Apparently, if you're almost forty, never married with no kids, then you've missed the point of life. I think I missed the point a long time ago. Maybe not wanting less than Mr. Right is no longer in style.

If only those people who want so

desperately to find you that perfect guy would take a moment to realize that you've already been searching and he's just not out there.

As I stood in my closet looking for something to wear to go out with a guy that I'd never met before, I wondered why. Why would I let Mona of all people talk me into a double date with guys I'd never met before and the only description she provided was that they looked like Greek Gods? Why could I not just call in sick? Why couldn't I just curl up on my sofa with a nice bottle of wine and watch a great movie?

I didn't have the answer. What I did know is that if I didn't go, Mona would never let me hear the end of it. So I found a tastefully sexy black dress and black pumps to wear and left to meet Mona at her gallery. By the time I arrived, Mona was already dressed in a too short dress that left no room to breathe.

"I'm going to regret this aren't I?" I asked with concern in my eyes.

"Girl why?" Mona replied. "We are young . . . ish . . . and out here getting our lives. There are two fine men waiting for us. They're going to feed us and we're going to party and have a good time. See, no need for regret."

I cut my eyes at Mona knowing that something was going to go wrong. It always does. We slowly walked the two blocks to the restaurant because Mona said the guys needed to see us as we walked in.

"It adds to the mystique," she said.

But when we arrived at the restaurant, our dates were not there. So, with the whole mystique thing out the window, we had the hostess seat us at a table in clear view of the front door and ordered some drinks.

I looked at my watch. Thirty minutes had gone by and the guys still were not there. Mona seemed unbothered as she read through the menu and moved her shoulders to the soft jazz music playing in the background.

"Um . . . where are your friends?" I asked.

"Girl who knows," Mona replied as if being late was a normal thing.

"Well shouldn't you call them and let them know that we're waiting on them?" I asked again.

"I guess," Mona replied as she took her phone out of her purse and began to text.

A couple of seconds later her phone beeped and she looked at it with a grin. "Oh see, they said they're having car trouble and should be here in a few," Mona explained.

I was frustrated. Promptness and having reliable transportation were on my list and this guy had now officially failed to meet those standards.

"Well, I'm hungry so I'm going to order something to eat," I said to Mona, who seemed completely preoccupied with whatever was going on with her phone.

After we were done eating, our dates still hadn't arrived. I looked at my watch again and then threw my napkin on the table. I was done with this so-called double date.

"I know, I know. Let me text them again and see what's going on," Mona said.

I turned my head in disgust as I signaled the waitress for the check.

"Oh, they said their car broke down by the club, so they'll just meet us there. Are you ready?" Mona said as she grabbed her purse.

"No, Mona, I'm ready to go home. You know good and well I do not do this," I said.

"And that's your problem; you never just go with the flow. So they didn't show up; that's not your man. We're just out to have a good time. Let's go to this club and have a good time," Mona proclaimed.

"This is not my definition of a good time, Mona. You go to the club. I'm going home," I said.

I got up and walked to my car, which was parked outside of Mona's gallery. Mona followed closely behind me.

"Okay, I'm sorry the night was a bust for you," Mona said.

"It's okay; the food was pretty good," I responded with a smile.

Mona smiled back and replied, "I just want you to get all these preconceived notions out of your head. People aren't perfect; life isn't perfect. I mean, shit happens; you just have to let go just a little bit to experience life just as it is Ruth."

I smiled knowingly at Mona and gave her a hug. I then got into my car and tried two times to start it before it finally started on the third try.

"You need a new car, Ruth," Mona said with a chuckle.

"I know. I just can't seem to find the time to go to a dealership," I said.

The moment the words came out of my mouth, Mona's face lit up with excitement.

"Oh my God, that sounds like an outing! Do you know how many guys be at a dealership?" Mona said as her eyes danced around in her head. "I'll plan the whole thing girl. I'll call you!" Mona took off running to her car before I could say anything.

I got home and opened the door to my quiet townhouse and walked in. I was so glad to be home. I don't know why I expect that at some point these dates would become magical and I would find the man of my dreams only to come home alone and disappointed. I stood in the hallway and began to take off my shoes. Before I could make my way to my bedroom to finish undressing, I heard the sound of the saxophone again. This time it seemed to be calling out to me.

I walked barefoot onto my back porch and sat on the swing chair and stared into the direction of the saxophone sound. The melody seemed to wrap its arms around me ever so gently and refused to let go. I didn't want it to. I rocked to the rhythm closing my eyes and allowing it to consume my soul.

"Why didn't you tell me you wanted to be set up on a date? I have the perfect guy for you," Gloria said after I told her about my and Mona's so-called double date.

I buried my face in my head as I sat at her kitchen island. If I had to hear one more person say that they have the perfect guy for me, I might've exploded. Every guy can't be that damn perfect for me otherwise I wouldn't be single.

"I wasn't looking to be set up," I replied. "I just wanted to go out for the night and have a good time."

"So, what you're telling me is that

Mona can hook you up with a guy but I can't?" Gloria replied as she stood on the other side of the kitchen island with her hand on her hip.

"Oh my God. That's not what I'm saying at all. I just wanted one night of nice music, good food and great conversation," I replied.

"And you thought Mona could find you a guy that could give you that?" she asked.

"I don't know. I just . . . I mean . . ."

"But I can," Gloria interrupted with a big grin on her face.

"What?" I asked confused.

"You just go home, change and be back here later tonight. I promise you an evening of nice music, good food and great conversation and you may just find your Mr. Right all in one night," Gloria grabbed hold of my arm and began leading me toward the back door.

She opened the door and ushered me to the other side.

"But . . . wait . . . what . . ." Everything was moving so fast I didn't know how to say no and that I'd rather be at home.

"Trust me!" she shouted before closing the door in my face.

It must have been close to seven that evening when I arrived back at Gloria's house. Every fiber in my body was telling me this was a bad idea. It was one of those been there done that type of things. I knew how the night was going to end; the perfect guy turns out not to be so perfect.

I reluctantly rang the doorbell and Charlie, Gloria's husband, opened it. He had a smirk on his face as he gave me a hug. He whispered in my ear, "I tried to stop her."

I chuckled and looked at him, "I'm sure you did, nothing can stop her."

"You're right about that," Charlie replied with loud laughter.

Just then Gloria came from around the corner and yelled out my name. She then grabbed my hand and led me into the living room. Sitting there was a fairly attractive man wearing what looked to be a custom-made brown suit. He stood up the moment we entered the living room and looked to be a little under six feet.

Gloria stood between us and said, "Donald, this is Ruth, one of my very best friends and Ruth, this is Donald. He's our accountant."

An accountant! I so badly wanted to

shout at Gloria. Most accountants I know are dry and boring. Gloria promised me great conversation and I didn't think I was going to get it. But since I was there, I figured I might as well play along.

I reached out my hand to meet his and said, "Nice to meet you, Donald."

"Likewise," he replied.

"Well . . . good," Gloria said trying to cut the tension. "How about you two have a seat and I'll, we'll go and check on dinner," she pulled Charlie behind her and left Donald and I alone in the living room.

It was really awkward. We just sat there staring in the air for a few minutes before finally he asked, "So, what do you do?"

"I'm a financial analyst," I replied.

"Oh, that's why Gloria wanted us to meet, the whole accountant and financial analyst thing. Guess she figured we'll have that in common," he said.

"Guess so," I replied still not seeing or feeling the connection.

I prayed that Gloria and Charlie would come into the living room quickly. This Donald guy seemed like a nice enough guy, but he just was not it for me. He kept trying to ask me questions but I kept giving him one word answers; I was so not feeling him. It wasn't that he was a bad looking guy, as accountants go; he just wasn't my type. He had no charisma about him. I didn't laugh once while he talked, not even a little blush.

I just stared at him as he explained . . . I'm not really sure what he was talking about. His mouth just kept moving but my ears refused to catch the words that were coming out. I tried to smile and act interested but I just couldn't bare it. I excused myself and went into the kitchen to find Gloria.

"Seriously, you thought he would be a good match for me?" I asked her.

"At least he showed up. That's better than the guy Mona found for you," she replied.

I squinted my eyes at her in frustration, ready to unload on her. Charlie must have sensed it because he said, "How about I go keep Donald company while you ladies figure this out."

"You have to stop being so picky," Gloria said.

"I'm not being picky," I replied.

"You're not even giving him a chance," she responded.

"I don't need to know a guy's whole life story to know he's not the one," I said.

"Okay, and that's fine. Let's just have dinner and we'll see," she said.

As I was thinking about staying, Charlie came back into the kitchen and said, "Hey, um, Donald wants to know if you knew all his food allergies?"

That was all I needed to hear. Anyone with a lot of food allergies is definitely too much work. I can't deal with a man who needs to be babied.

I tucked my purse under my arm and headed for the back door.

"Where are you going?" Gloria asked.

"Home," I replied.

"That's just rude," she said as I opened the door.

"No it's not!" I yelled as I walked through the door, waiving bye.

I got back home and lied down on the sofa staring at the ceiling. At some point you have to come to the realization that there is no perfect person for you, and I think I've reached that point.

I closed my eyes tightly and tried to fight the disappointment of what life had presented. Just then, I heard the saxophone playing again. This time it seemed to be calling out my name. I walked out on my back porch and sat on my swing. The connection that I had with that saxophone seemed to be the only connection I was ever meant to have.

I can remember when I was growing up, my parents seemed to have that effortless type of love. The kind that seemed to know what the other is thinking or feeling without words being spoken. The kind that comforted and wiped away tears. The kind that made the other laugh with just a gesture. The kind that I never seemed to find except when I'm listening to the saxophone. It made me feel like every song was just for me. Like it knew just what I was feeling and wanted to make all my fears and doubts go away.

A part of me felt silly putting all my expectations of what love should be on an instrument, but this instrument spoke to a part of me that I know was only meant for the man who was supposed to love me.

It had been a few weeks since I walked out on Gloria and her so-called perfect man for me. She hadn't called or texted and I'd been too afraid to call her. I did feel bad about the way I left, but I'm just so tired of people always saying they have the perfect man for me only to end up with a dud.

The truth is I don't even know the perfect guy for me. I used to. I had all these preconceived notions in my head of how he should look, act, walk, talk, all the good stuff. But every time I think I've found him, it just all goes to hell. I don't want to be that girl all alone with nothing to show for her life. But I also don't want to be that girl hanging on to any man because of that fear. It's just the worse space to be in. So it's probably time to give up and let life unfold as it may.

All those great romance stories say that Mr. Right will somehow come and find you, like he's just going to drop out of the sky. Maybe it will happen that way for me.

I sat at my dining room table playing with the handle of my coffee mug, realizing that I'm almost forty and there is no great romance for me, at least none that has happened yet. Life is funny. When you say to yourself, *no love life for me, I'm building my career*, that's when the flood gates of men come pouring through and at that moment everyone wants you. But when you're finally ready to settle down and build a family, NOTHING, not even one decent man with just a slight bit of potential, just enough for you to work with.

Seems like every man wants younger, perkier, cuter. I'm older, wiser and still cute as hell but NOTHING. Clearly I've made some missteps along the way. Before I could dwindle in self-loathing, the doorbell rang and on the other end was Mona and Gloria. The moment I saw Gloria, I grabbed her and gave her a hug. "Are you still mad at me?" I asked.

"Not as much as I was when you stormed out my house leaving me to come up with an excuse to tell Donald," Gloria replied.

"What did you end up saying?" I asked.

"That you got a rash," she replied with a smirk.

"What!" I yelled.

"Well he understood, halfway through dinner his face broke out . . . I didn't know people could be allergic to salt," she explained.

"Oh my God," I said shaking my head, realizing that I made the right decision.

"What kinda boy in the bubble did you try to hook her up with?" Mona asked.

"At least he showed up," Gloria answered.

"Did you guys come over just to show me how pathetic my love life is?" I asked.

"No, we did not," Mona answered. "We came to take you car shopping."

"What? Today?" I was not in the mood to go car shopping.

Mona was always looking for something to do. If you said you got a tear on blouse, that's a trip to the mall to buy a whole new wardrobe. If you said your milk went bad, that's a trip to the grocery store to buy two shopping carts full of food. My car was a mess but buying a new one was not in my plans for the day.

"Charlie said that there's a new dealership that just opened and they're having some great deals," Gloria added.

"Yup, so get dressed," Mona said as she pushed me toward my room. I reluctantly obeyed.

The dealership was packed with people. I guess everyone had heard about the deals that they were having. At first the three of us just walked around looking at the different cars, then Mona decided to jump in and out of the cars pretending to be driving while the car was in park. That must've gotten the salesman's attention because he started to walk right up to us. At first, from a distance, he looked like some ordinary man in a suit. But then he got closer and I realized that he was my ex, Brandon. Our breakup was the worse. Hell, our relationship wasn't that great either.

In the beginning I thought that he could be the one. He was charismatic, attentive and driven. All the things I look for in a man. But I found out pretty quickly that he was charismatic, attentive and driven to a whole host of other women. There were girls everywhere. When we went out to eat there was one; when we went to the movies there was one. Hell, we even went to his mother's house and a girl was waiting for him in the driveway.

Clearly he was not the "let's get married and have some babies" type. I was just glad to get the cheater out of my life. The last thing I wanted was to see or talk to him.

"Hello ladies," Brandon said with a big smile on his face.

I couldn't tell if he recognized us, well me, or if it was his normal salesman charm. But Mona jumped out the car she was sitting in and said, "Well if it isn't dirty dog, Brandon."

"Mona, always interesting to see you," Brandon replied. Then he turned to me and said, "Hey Ruth, it's been a long time. How have you been?"

"She's not being cheated on," Mona chimed in.

"Um, Mona, how about we go look at

some other cars down that way," Gloria said as she grabbed Mona's arm and pushed her away. "Great seeing you again, Brandon."

"Same here," Brandon said to Gloria.

I smiled at Brandon, remembering how charming he could be and hoping not to get sucked back into his web.

"Hey," I said.

"So, are you going to answer me?" he asked with a smile.

"About what?"

"How have you been?"

"Oh . . . yeah . . . good . . . great . . . work is good . . . life good . . . everything is great," I replied.

Brandon let out a loud hardy laugh and said, "Same old Ruth."

I didn't know what he meant by that and I didn't really care to ask. I figured any minute now a bunch of women would be falling out the sky and I wanted to get away from him before that happened.

"So, you're shopping for a car?" he asked.

"Yeah, nothing fancy, just something . . ." I lost my voice for a moment. My thoughts were not processing. The sun beamed down and hit Brandon's fingers and blinged. He had on a ring, not just any ring, but a wedding ring. He had gotten married. The man who couldn't stay faithful to me for one second had gotten married.

"Ruth? Are you ok?" he asked.

"Um, you're married," I said.

"Oh yeah," he looked at his finger and smiled. Not just any smile but one of those admiration and fulfillment type of smiles.

He wasn't just married; he was happily married. What happened to that endless stream of women? All of a sudden he's a one-woman man? For some reason I found myself getting angry and I didn't know why. We were over a long time ago and it was one of those good ridden types of over. So why was I so upset that he was married?

"Congratulations," I mustered up the nerve to say. "Who's the lucky lady? I hope it's not one of the many women who called my phone?" That probably wasn't very nice but being nice wasn't in me at that moment. This man who I thought would be my husband, if he could get his act together, had managed to get his act together for another woman. So, what the hell did I do wrong?

Brandon smiled, "No. I met her after we, well you know. She's an amazing person."

"Well, that's great." I gave Brandon a

weak thumbs up and tried to pull myself together. I didn't want him to know how pissed I was that he hadn't chosen me.

The rest of the time with Brandon seemed awkward. He did help me find a pretty great car but I found myself not being able to get over this anger I was feeling about him being married. I felt like there was more I wanted to say to him but I didn't know what that was. I didn't know how to put into words how I was feeling. Maybe I was angrier at myself than at him. After all people do move on after a breakup.

"You probably just didn't get closure," Gloria said as we sat on my balcony later that evening.

"What closure? I hated being in a relationship with him," I responded.

"You probably just want to know if

she's cuter than you," Mona added.

"I could care less what she looks like," I answered.

"Then what is it, Ruth?" Gloria asked.

"I don't know," I replied. "Maybe it's because he's married and I'm not. I mean, is it really that easy for guys? They can sleep with a hundred women, but they'll still be married before forty."

"Wait, is that what all of this is about?" Gloria asked. "You've got the bug?"

"What bug?" I asked.

"The marriage bug," Gloria answered.

"Oh, a couple of nights out with me and that will be cured," Mona said.

"I don't . . . I'm not. I have no idea what I've got. I just don't know what's going on with my life," I said.

"There's nothing wrong with your life; your guy just hasn't found you yet, but he's coming," Gloria said.

"He finds you at twenty. At our ages if you haven't been found by then, you just need to stay hidden because clearly something is wrong with you," I told Gloria.

"That's not true," Gloria said. "The question you should be asking yourself is are you ready to be found."

"What kind of question is that Gloria?" Mona asked.

"A genuine one," Gloria answered.

I sat back and looked up at the sky thinking about Gloria's question. Maybe that was my problem; maybe I wasn't ready to be found. But how do I even begin the process of getting ready?

Just then the saxophone began to play, as if on cue.

"What's that?" Mona asked.

"My new neighbor," I replied.

"That's nice," Gloria said as the three of us sat back and enjoyed the sound.

Even though the three of us were sitting there, it felt like the saxophone was playing only for me, the sound was made just for my ears alone. It was as if the saxophone was having a conversation with my heart, telling me that everything was going to be alright, that it was with me. I listened closely to the musical words and felt comforted. I smiled to myself, trusting in those words and letting it take care of my fears.

Am I ready to be found? That question had consumed me every single day since

Gloria asked it. How would someone even know when they're ready to be found? Is it a feeling? Does your mind just click to a state of being ready? I don't have a clue, so maybe I'm not ready to be found. Maybe I never will be.

Who knows? I just want to stop driving myself crazy. If it's not going to happen, then I needed to accept it and move on. Life is what it is, and I just can't change it, even though sometimes I wished I could.

I pulled my brand-new car up to Mona's studio and she was waiting for me on the sidewalk with two cups of coffee. Mona got in excited. I'd promised her a ride in my new car and ever since I picked it up from the dealership, she'd been reminding me. I figured a ride around town was a great distraction.

"It's even prettier than I remembered,"

Mona said as she rubbed the seats and dashboard.

"It drives great," I added. "I'm in love with it."

"Here, I brought you coffee," Mona said.

She placed mine in the cup holder and held hers in her hand.

I drove off as we talked and laughed. But before we could get anywhere, Mona went to put her cup of coffee to her mouth and the lid flew off and coffee spilled all over her and my brand-new car.

I pulled over quickly as Mona yelled in pain but luckily for her, the coffee wasn't all that hot and she didn't get burned. But unlucky for me, my cloth beige seats were stained.

Mona shot out the car and tried to clean it with some napkins but that only made it worse.

"That's not working, Mona!" I yelled.

"I don't know what else to do," she answered in a panic.

"There's a car wash not far from my house; maybe they can get it out," I said.

I drove to the car wash as quickly as possible, praying that the stain wouldn't set in.

When we got there, a guy walked right up to us and asked if he could help us. There was something that felt familiar about him. His eyes were warm and inviting and he looked at me as if I was an old friend, like he was happy to see me.

"Coffee spilled on my seat; can you get it out?" I said to him.

He opened my passenger door and looked closely at the stain.

"Yeah, we should be able to take care of

it," he said.

Then he signaled and a teenage boy ran over. He told the boy to take my car for detailing. I reluctantly gave my car keys over and wondered if there was anyone older but when I looked around, there were only teenage boys.

The young man took my car and we followed the guy into the office. As I was handling payment, Mona was looking around and noticed that work was being done on the car wash.

"Who's your contractor?" she asked.

"That would be me," the man answered.

"Do you only do your own work or are you open for clients?" Mona asked again.

"We are open for clients. Are you looking for a contractor?" the man asked.

"Yes, I am. I'm adding on to my studio. Maybe you can stop by and give me an estimate," Mona responded.

"Absolutely, here's my card. Give me a call and we can set up a time." The man handed Mona a white card with the name Bo written on it. Then he left to check on my car.

"He's cute," Mona said.

"I'm not speaking to you," I replied.

"Oh calm down, cutie pie. Bo is making everything all better. Besides I'll pay you back when we get to my studio," she said.

I cut my eyes at her and turned to watch Bo from the window. He was cute. He had that man's man type of vibe. The type that plays cards and watches football and fixes things around the house. I like those type of guys. But one that works at a car wash? Not for me. He probably has roommates or worse, lives with his mother in the basement. Probably has a couple of baby mommas all over the city. Probably even been to jail three or four times.

"He is gorgeous," Mona said as she snuck up behind me.

"Yeah, you always did like a project," I replied.

"How you figured he's a project?" she asked.

"Look at where we're standing," I answered.

Mona shook her head and replied, "That's your problem, Ruth. You judge people too quickly."

"I do not," I proclaimed. "Besides, it doesn't matter what I think; if you're interested, go for it."

"I don't think he's interested in me," she said.

"And why do you say that?" I asked.

"Didn't you see the way he kept looking

at you? That man is into you," she answered.

"Well the feeling is not mutual," I said.

Bo came back in the office a few minutes later and handed me my car keys. He also gave me his card and said that I should call him if I needed anything else. I'm sure I won't but I didn't tell him that. Besides, I just wanted to get out of there. Mona's annoying "I told you so" grin was starting to get on my nerves.

As I got into my car, I balled up Bo's business card and threw it into the glove compartment. My eyes met Mona's disappointed stare. But I didn't care one bit. What do I look like dating a car wash guy? He probably didn't have any goals or vision or any purpose for his life. Guys like that come into a woman's life and completely destroy it. That was not happening to me, no matter how gorgeous the guy was.

"Ruth, are you going to eat or are you just going to sit there and play with your food?" Mona asked me.

The weeks since running into Brandon had been some of the most confusing. I kept wondering how a guy who couldn't even commit to where we were going for dinner was all of a sudden reformed and happily married. Did he just wake up one day and decide that it was a good day to get married? If our relationship had lasted just a few more months, would we have been married? I literally didn't get it and something in me wanted to know so badly.

"Are you alright, Ruth?" Gloria asked.

"I guess," I replied still trying to

organize all the thoughts that were swimming around in my head.

"You don't seem okay," Gloria replied. "You've been acting weird for a few days."

"I don't know. I mean . . . do you guys think Brandon and I had something real or was it just that superficial placeholder until the right person came along?" I glanced at Mona and Gloria and they seemed baffled by my question.

"Why are you asking? Don't tell me you're still hung up on that cheater," Mona responded.

"No, I just find it weird that he's married and I'm just here, still looking," I replied.

"Not everyone is meant for each other, Ruth," Gloria said, "Some relationships are just lessons."

"Is that what that was?" I replied. "I

mean, him getting married just didn't fit his type?"

"Type? What type?" Gloria asked.

"Girl, you know good and well there are different types of men and I'm with Ruth; Brandon was the forever playa type," Mona added.

"Well, I don't know about the different types of men, but I do believe that there is someone for everyone. I think Brandon just found his someone," Gloria replied.

"Nope, I don't buy that," Mona said. "People don't just bump into someone and like magic that's the one. Guys don't know you're the one until you tell them or they run out of options."

"Okay, I was with you until the end, Mona," I replied with a smile.

"Seriously. You could date a guy for like ever and until every other girl turns them down, they will not commit," Mona explained.

"Damn, skeptical much?" Gloria added.

"Okay, let's put it to a test," Mona said and started looking around the restaurant. She saw a couple sitting together and lovingly talking.

Before Gloria or I could stop her, she jumped up and went over to them. Their table was not far from where we were sitting and Mona was not trying to use her discreet voice. We heard her ask the couple if they were together and if they were married. The girl said they were dating and had been for about eight months. Then Mona asked the man, "Is she the one?"

"Excuse me?" The man responded confused by Mona's boldness.

"Is she the one? Are you planning on marrying her?" Mona asked again.

"I don't think that's any of your business," the man replied.

"Oh, come on, I just want to know if she meets all the qualifications of being your wife, assuming you have some?"

"Ma'am can you please go back to your table," the man said.

"Why is it so hard for you to answer?" Mona insisted then turned to the woman and asked, "Wouldn't you like to know?"

The woman sat back in her chair and looked at the man intensely, "Yes, I would."

"Baby, are you seriously going to let some stranger into our relationship?" the man asked.

Gloria and I held our breaths; we were mortified. Mona stood there with pure joy all over her face.

"Fine," the man said. "I don't know yet.

There are some things that we need to work on first."

"Things like what?" the woman asked.

"Like this, you just let some stranger get you all riled up. That's the same thing that happens with your family; they're all in our business," the man explained.

"So you don't want to marry me because of my family?" the woman shouted and then stood up to leave.

The man quickly stood up and threw cash on the table to pay for their meal. Then he ran out the restaurant after her.

Mona came back to the table with a huge smile on her face.

"Are you insane?" Gloria asked.

"No, I'm realistic. That poor girl would be thinking that one day he's going to wake up and like magic she'll be his someone," Mona explained. "But clearly she's not."

"If your theory is true Mona, then what you've proven is that there's something wrong with me. That guys don't commit to me because I have the issue," I said.

"Well do you?" Mona asked.

"Mona!" Gloria shouted.

"No, I think we're on to something," Mona said as she leaned in to me. "Ruth, have you asked guys why the relationship didn't work?"

"No, who does that?" I answered.

"You should, and you should start with Brandon," Mona replied with a smirk and one raised eyebrow.

Part 2:

Character

J.E. Smythe

I sat in my car for what seemed like forever. I watched as people walked in and out of the dealership. My nerves didn't allow me to step out of my car. I started second guessing Mona's ridiculous plan. I didn't know how I could just walk up to Brandon and ask, "So, why did you cheat on me?" He would think that I'd absolutely lost my mind.

Maybe I had. I don't even remember why I'd hung on to him for so long and it's not that I wanted him back; I guess I just needed to know why this woman was wife material and I wasn't. I mean, we were good in the beginning, at least I thought so. There were moments when I thought that Brandon could be the one, moments when I thought that if I hang on, be the understanding girlfriend, that he would change and see that I was the one. That didn't happen. I wasn't the one for him and I can see now that he wasn't the one for me.

It's not that I think I'm perfect or anything, I'm sure I have my short comings, but I was in it for the long haul with Brandon. I put everything I had into our relationship. So where did it all go wrong? Where did I go wrong?

Brandon & Ruth

The hardware store was so out of my element, but Mona and I had talked to this happily married woman some nights before who said that the best place to meet men were at car shows or hardware stores. Since no car shows were going on, I guess the hardware store was the spot. I wore my tight jeans, face full of makeup, and hair fresh from the salon. I weaved in and out of aisles hoping someone would see me or I'd see someone worth approaching. The store wasn't entirely packed but there were a few guys roaming around, just none that stood out. Then I saw him, in the lightbulb aisle. Tall, dark and perfectly built.

I pulled my shopping cart close but not too close for him to know that I was watching him. I looked up and down the shelves and acted like I didn't know which lightbulb to buy. I stood there for a while hoping he'd get the hint, and he did.

He walked up behind me and said, "That one is the best brand."

I turned to face him and he looked even better up close than he did from far away. I almost couldn't speak. His smile would make any woman want to throw herself at him. I had to catch myself. He had charisma written all over him, and he knew it.

"Hi, I'm Brandon," he said as he extended his hand toward mine.

"Hi, I'm Ruth," I replied meeting his hand. "Thank you for the suggestion."

I picked up the lightbulb he suggested and started to walk away, slowly of course so that he could still stop me, and he did.

"Um, Ruth, it would seem almost criminal to meet someone as beautiful as you and not ask you out, or at least for your phone number." His smile was everything in that moment.

Obviously, I gave Brandon my number. If he hadn't asked, I probably would've thrown it at him.

I went home and waited not so patiently for his call. As the day went on, I thought that maybe he'd decided he wasn't interested after all. I picked up the phone and called Gloria.

"I can't believe you followed that crazy lady's advice," Gloria said after I had explained everything to her.

"But it worked, I think, I hope."

"Girl, you know the last time I picked a guy up from a hardware store, I literally picked him up because his ass didn't have a car."

"Well that's not the issue here."

"How do you know that? You don't even know if he has a girlfriend or worse, if he's married."

"He's not married; I don't think. I didn't see a ring, okay. So maybe I should have asked more questions before giving him my number. But you should have seen him, Gloria."

"I'm going to stop preaching to you and Mona about how true love works; there's no point. You guys rather listen to some random stranger who says to go to the hardware store and there he'll be."

"I know it's not that easy but . . ." I stopped mid-sentence to look at my phone because it had beeped from an incoming call. "Gloria hold on a sec; I'm getting another call." I clicked over and said hello.

"Hello, may I speak to Ruth?" A deep, sexy male voice said on the other end.

I just knew it was Brandon. My whole body tingled with excitement.

"This is Ruth," I said joyfully.

"Hi beautiful, this is Brandon." His voice made me melt. It was so inviting and lingered on my ears.

"Hi, can you hold one moment?"

I quickly clicked over to Gloria and shouted, "It's him!"

"Are you serious?"

"Yes, I am. I'll call you back and fill you in, bye." I quickly hung up on Gloria, not giving her a chance to respond, and clicked back over to Brandon. I couldn't wait to hear that voice again.

"I'm sorry about that," I said. "I was talking to someone on the other line."

"If you can't talk right now, I can call you back later."

"Oh no, I can talk."

"Great, because I couldn't wait to talk to you again."

I could feel myself blushing. This man was incredible. I wanted to know everything about him but most importantly,

I wanted to know why it took him so long to come into my life.

"You know, I don't know anything about you; where are you from?"

"Born and raised in the Queen City."

"Okay, what do you do for a living?"

"I sell cars. What else do you want to know?"

I wanted so badly to shout out, how many kids do you have? Are you married? Have a girlfriend? Baby mamas? Instead I held my composure; I really didn't want to scare him off.

"A lot," I said with a slight giggle, "but I'm not sure if you have the time right now."

Brandon chuckled and replied, "I'll tell you one interesting fact about me; I'm a damn good cook."

"Are you really?"

"I sure am. How about you come over tonight and I can cook for you? We can get to know each other better. I promise I'm not a crazy killer."

I smiled and replied, "Isn't that what a crazy killer would say?"

"Probably," Brandon said with laughter, "but I honestly give you my word that I'm harmless. We can leave the front door and all the windows open."

"Okay, I'd love for you to cook for me tonight." How could anyone turn down that charm?

"Great. I'll text you my address, can't wait to see you tonight Ruth."

When I hung up the phone, I felt like a middle school girl whose first crush had just looked in her direction and smiled. There was something about Brandon that made me feel excited.

The anticipation of seeing Brandon lasted throughout the day. When the time finally came, all the nerves kicked in. I started to second guess everything, from my hairstyle to my dress choice and even the heals I wore. I wanted Brandon to look at me in amazement, like I was the only woman in the world.

When he opened the door, his eyes lit up, and I can tell he was pleased with what he saw. It wasn't to the level I wanted but I could work with it.

He went all out for the dinner. His apartment was filled with scented candles and flowers and the softest, most romantic music. The food was almost as if it had come from a high-end restaurant.

I couldn't remember ever being treated that way by a guy, so I stayed the night with him and every night after. We were stuck together like glue and everything he asked of me I did.

In my mind, he had to be the one. The feelings I had for him were so passionate and intense that I couldn't imagine myself feeling that way about any other guy. I never wanted those feelings to go away; I didn't want him to go away. My life became about Brandon and everything I did I did for him, for us.

Mona and Gloria didn't trust him; basically, Mona couldn't stand him. She would always say, "I just get this vibe from him."

"What are you talking about? What kinda vibe?" I would ask her.

"You know, the kinda vibe that makes your antenna go up, like he's up to something. Like he needs to be followed or you may need to go through his phone; you know what I mean, Ruth. Something just isn't right about that dude," she would explain.

"You sound crazy. There is nothing strange about my man. He's good; we're good." I would tell her.

And we were good, for a while. Then things started to change and that stupid antenna going up thing that Mona was talking about started to happen to me; antennas were going up all over the damn place.

Brandon began showing up to our dates late. He wouldn't call as frequently as he used to and when he did, our conversations began to get shorter and shorter.

One night I sat him down to ask him what was going on; I was fed up and ready to walk. But he was as smooth as ever and said, "I'm just busy with work; you got to trust me baby. This isn't going to work if you don't."

So I chose to trust him and I let it go. I felt like we had something special and that this relationship was the right one for me and I didn't want to mess it up. But all of a sudden it was like women were crawling out from everywhere. There were girls calling his phone, they were coming up to us while we were out to dinner, and they were even calling my phone. One day one girl came to my house looking for him. When I told her that he didn't live there, this girl had the nerves to say, "Well, when you see him, tell him Titi looking for him."

I was beyond pissed. The moment he walked through the door I shouted, "What the hell is a Titi and why the hell did she come to my door looking for you?"

But he'd just keep saying that nothing is

going on and to trust him. He said that he wasn't with any of those girls. Even though everything in me said that he was a low-down dirty dog, I still hung on to him and did everything I could to be with him.

That was until the low-down dirty dog came by my house one night. He was looking good and smooth as always, so I thought that he had something special planned. But I was sadly mistaken.

He walked in, gave me a kiss and said, "Hey baby, how are you doing tonight?"

Something in his tone sounded off, so I didn't respond right away. Then he said, "Come on let's sit for a minute."

He grabbed hold of my hands as we sat on my sofa and continued, "I just feel like I need to be honest with you. I think we have something great going on but I'm just not in a space where I want to settle down. I think

we should still keep what we got but leave ourselves free to see other people."

I pulled my hand away from him fast. I couldn't believe he had the nerves to come into my home with that bullshit.

"Haven't you been seeing people already!" I yelled out.

"What do you mean?" He asked then quickly waved the question away. "Baby listen, this is just how it has to be for me right now. You can either roll with it or we can be done."

I looked away from him and nodded my head. "We can be done," I replied. Then I got up and showed him the door.

As he passed by me to leave, a look of confusion filled his face, as if he had expected me to have a different response. But I was done. I slammed the door on him, his women and all his doggish ways.

So why was I sitting outside his job? I had no idea. Mona's crazy ideas should never be followed, and I should know better than to listen to her. Thoughts of Brandon yelling at me and shouting "you crazy psycho!" kept replaying in my head. I could also hear him telling me to get over it and that he never really wanted me anyway; I was just someone to fill his time. That probably would've been the hardest to hear. What girl wants to hear that the man she once loved didn't feel the same way about her? I realized in that instant that coming to see Brandon was definitely a bad idea.

Just as I started my car to leave, there was a knock on the passenger side window. It was Brandon. My nerves went into overdrive. I rolled down my window and said, "Hi".

"Hey," he replied. "Is everything alright?"

"Um . . . yeah . . . no . . . do you have a moment to talk?" I answered.

"Sure, do you want to come inside?"

"No. Do you mind getting in the car? I promise it won't take long."

Brandon looked around him first and then got into my car almost reluctantly. My breath got heavy and harder to leave my body. My hands became sweaty and my mouth became dry.

But it was too late to change my mind. He was sitting in my car staring at me waiting for me to speak. To say something logical as to why I was at his job asking him to get into my car. I had to pull myself together and say something.

"This is strange, huh?" I asked with a nervous grin.

"Kinda. What's going on?" He turned his whole body toward me and stared at me intently.

"So, I was thinking, we broke up and I thought that you were this unredeemable dog, who will forever be chasing girls," I started to explain.

Brandon let out a loud laugh and threw his head back. "Yeah, I can't deny that I had that issue."

"Right, but that's not who you are, at least not now," I said.

"Where are you going with this Ruth?" he asked.

"For a moment I could explain away our break up by blaming it on you and saying that you could never be faithful . . ." I said.

"Ruth, I'm still a little confused," he interrupted.

"Okay, so, I guess what I'm asking you is why couldn't you be this guy for me? I mean . . . just, why not me?" I asked.

I sat back and waited for Brandon to laugh in my face. To tell me that I was being ridiculous, that this whole thing was the most insane thing that had ever taken place for him. But he didn't; he sat back and looked straight ahead. For a moment there was an awkward silence and I wanted to tell him to forget about it, to just forget that I was ever there.

"Ruth, I don't know if I have an answer for you." The words came out of Brandon's lips, but his face said different.

I could tell he was holding back, maybe he didn't want to hurt my feelings or maybe he didn't find it important enough, but there

was definitely something he was holding back.

"I kinda do, Brandon. It's been eating me up. Please, be honest with me," I told him.

Brandon turned back to me and placed a soft smile on his face. I secretly hoped that he would charm his way out of this, but I knew that he needed to tell me the truth and I needed to hear it.

"Ruth, you are an incredible woman. Sometimes things just don't work out," he said.

"I know that, Brandon, but there has to be a reason. Just tell me," I responded.

"Um, when I was with you, I was in a different space. I just wanted to be with a whole lot of women," Brandon said.

"So, you didn't feel the same way I felt in the relationship, or at least didn't take it

as seriously as I did?" I asked.

"I don't think it was that simple for me. At first it was all good, I mean you're a special woman," Brandon answered.

"So, something changed?" I continued to ask.

"I wouldn't say that; I was always that guy who liked being with a bunch of women. I just didn't know if you were that girl who would let me," he explained.

"I don't understand what you mean," I said.

"When I met my wife, she reminded me of you; she was tough, smart and beautiful. We went out one day while we were still dating and well one of my friends came up to us . . ." Brandon started to explain.

"You mean one of your women?" I said sarcastically.

"Yeah, and I expected my wife to throw

a fit and then I'll talk her down, and we'll be all good," he said.

"Sorta like our routine?"

"Exactly," Brandon said. "But she didn't. After I dropped her home, she got out the car and calmly thanked me for dinner. After that nothing. She didn't answer my calls, didn't open the door when I stopped by, and all my gifts and flowers were returned. This went on for months until finally I ran into her at a friend's party and she told me that there was no room in her life for me and all my women. Right then and there I realized that she was it for me; I had to stop being that guy to be with her. In the time that she was freezing me out, all I could do was think of her. No other woman even came close and the thought of living my life without her was unbearable."

I started to play back everything he was saying, but it wasn't making sense. I didn't see myself as the type of woman who would allow a man to cheat. I never gave him permission to cheat. Not once did I say I was alright with it. What was the difference between what I did and what she did?

"So you're saying we should have broken up sooner?" I asked, feeling the anger building up.

"No, I mean . . . I don't know. It was just too easy with you. You made yourself too available. I went out and did my dirt and came back and told you everything was clean, and you accepted it. I guess I needed you to put your foot down a bit more. Require me to be a better man. I don't know if any of this is making any sense," Brandon said.

I sat back in my chair and turned away. I guess that I never considered that me trying to be the understanding and trusting girlfriend was a permission slip to cheat. I thought that's what guys wanted. A girl that's a rider that would be there no matter what. That won't let anyone come between them. I tried to be that for Brandon, but I guess that wasn't enough.

Brandon kept telling me how sorry he was, but I wasn't in the right mental space to hear him. He got out the car and I drove away more confused than when I arrived. Was I the girl that allowed her man to treat her any kinda way? I didn't think I was. At least, I didn't want to be.

I took my time getting home. By the time I did, it was already dark outside, and my townhouse had a greyish glare with a tranquil yet lonely feel. I poured myself a glass of wine and walked out to my back porch and sat on my swing chair. That one talk with Brandon made me begin to question the type of woman I thought I was or I thought I wanted to be. Was this my issue all along? Had I been allowing men to walk all over me as if it was acceptable, so much so that they lost respect for me?

I took a sip of my wine and lied down on the swing chair. Then, like as if on cue, I began to be serenaded by the sound of the mesmerizing saxophone that played in the house across the street. It filled me with peace and sang lovingly to the thoughts that ran through my mind.

Mona's studio was a mess. There were debris and tools everywhere. I walked in watching my every step. Some young teenager almost ran into me with a lug wrench in his hand. I yelled out Mona's name so loud that I think I scared the kid more than he scared me.

"What?" Mona yelled back.

"Where are you?" I asked.

"Back here, in my office!"

"How the hell do I get back there?" I asked out loud to myself.

"Let me help you," a male voice said from behind me.

I turned around and saw the man from the car wash standing behind me wearing a white, half sweaty wife beater. His muscles glistened from the top of his tattoo covered shoulders to the tip of his strong masculine fingers. The sight of him almost took my breath away and I had to catch myself.

"I'm sorry?" I asked not quite sure what

he said to me.

"I said let me help you," he replied. "There's a lot of stuff around; I don't want you to hurt yourself."

He reached out his hand and grabbed hold of mine. He pulled me cautiously behind him as we passed young men hammering away at walls and floors.

When we reached Mona, she looked up with so much joy on her face as if her whole studio was not caving in around her.

"Hey girl!" Mona shrieked.

"Hey girl?" I asked hugging her. "What in the world is going on?"

"You remember Bo from the car wash?" she replied. "Well, he has graciously been helping me expand my studio."

Bo smiled at her and said, "I'll leave you ladies alone."

As he walked out, Mona's eyes followed him and she said, "Oh Lord, that's a fine man."

I shook my head and folded my arms, remembering why I went to see her in the first place.

"So, I took your stupid advice," I said.

"None of my advice is stupid," she replied, "but which one?"

"The one about me going to see Brandon and asking him why we didn't work out," I told her.

"Oh my God, did you really? Tell me everything." Her face lit up and she began to smile from ear to ear.

"There's not much to tell," I replied as I started pacing around the room. "He said that I made myself too available. That I didn't put my foot down and make him stop cheating. As if I was a push over type of girlfriend."

"Well . . ." Mona replied.

"Well what?" I stopped pacing and looked at her.

"I'm not saying you're the reason he was a dog; hell, he was born that way," she responded. "But you were so into him that you sorta let him get away with a few things."

"Do you agree with him, that I'm some weak pushover type of woman?"

"No! That's not what I'm saying at all. Just relax. When you go to the next guy, maybe he'll clear it up for you," she said.

"Are you kidding me? I'm done with this," I told her.

"You can't be; you're just getting started. Besides how else are you going to know if there's a pattern that needs to be broken before you find your Mr. Right?"

Mona said.

I looked at her and rolled my eyes. "I'm going to stop listening to you," I said and walked out.

I could hear Mona yelling from behind me, "You'll thank me for this one day!"

Bo was kneeling on the floor just outside of Mona's office removing nails. I felt embarrassed thinking that he may have heard our conversation. I turned my face away from him and walked out, holding onto the wall as tightly as possible.

Later that night I sat at my kitchen table. The back window was open and the cool night air filled the room. I laid my phone on the table and stared at it for what seemed like forever. The saxophone sound in the distance seemed to give me courage.

I picked up the phone and dialed. I closed my eyes tightly as I anticipated the voice on the other end.

"Hello," the male voice answered.

"Hey, this is Ruth. I know it's been a long time and this may sound crazy, but can we meet and talk? There's something kinda important that I want to ask you."

Part 3:

Faith

The Eyes of Love

The Saturday early afternoon breeze ran past my face with ease as I nervously sat at the table outside of the restaurant. The palm of my hands filled with sweat. I held onto the white napkin on the table trying my best to wipe away the sweat and calm my nerves. So many thoughts were running through my head. I don't think I was prepared to hear the same thing I heard from Brandon. I don't think I was ready to know that I was a weak version of a woman. The type of woman that no man would take seriously.

Once again, I was wondering why I listened to Mona. It almost felt as if I was punishing myself. Why would anyone want to know why someone didn't want them? Most rational people just move on with their life, but here I was begging guys to tell me all the things that were wrong with me.

It was insane; I was insane. Maybe that's what's wrong with me, insanity. Problem solved. Maybe now I can stop this mess and head home or maybe make a quick trip to a therapist, or maybe I could just stop listening to Mona all together.

Everything in me said this was a bad idea. But there was this little annoying part that kept on saying that I needed to see it through and that part seemed to be the loudest.

I lowered my head in frustration, just wanting to shut up my mind and get up and leave. Then I heard a male voice say, "Hey Ruth."

I lifted my head to see this perfectly built male body that dripped with sex appeal from head to toe. I had forgotten how much he turned me on just by looking at him. Everything about him was perfection. From the dimples on his face to the way his pecs visibly flexed effortlessly under his shirt. The man was built to perfection.

"Hi Curtis," I said with a smile.

He smiled back and sat down across from me. The gentleness of his face had me wondering why I let him go. He was such a sweet and caring guy. I remembered him being attentive and warm. He was the quintessential gentle giant. He always called to ask me how my day was going and if I was eating right. He always seemed to have a smile on his face, so much so that I don't really remember ever asking him how his day was going. Guess I just assumed everything was going great with him.

Curtis & Ruth

Curtis was an interesting find. I don't think I ever really intended for us to be in it for the long haul. There was just no way I could deny him. He walked into the room with such a presence that a woman couldn't help but throw herself at him. He would smile at you and there was a peace that radiated from him.

"Wow, this is really nice," I said to Mona as we walked into the newly built gym.

It had every piece of workout equipment that you could possibly imagine.

It was huge and fairly full for a place that recently opened.

"I think we came to the right spot," Mona said as she ogled all the well-defined men that passed us.

A tall, tanned, muscular guy with a head full of blond hair approached us. He was wearing a t-shirt with the gym's name written on it. He smiled at Mona and me and said, "Good afternoon ladies. How may I help you?"

"You can give me your name and number," Mona said as he began to blush.

I shot Mona a look of aggravation and said to him, "Please ignore her; we would like to sign up."

"Absolutely, why don't you ladies follow me and we can get everything set up." He replied as he led us over to a small desk against the wall. "By the way, my name is Jake."

"And your number?" Mona blurted out.

"Mona!" I gave her a slight nudge as Jake smiled looking to be flattered.

We sat with Jake as he went through all the gym had to offer. Just before we signed on the dotted line, we learned that they offer one-on-one training at an additional cost of course.

Since I hadn't been to the gym in some time, I jumped at the chance. Mona refused saying her body was already perfectly trained and she wasted no time flaunting that body in front of Jake.

After I signed up for the one-on-one training, Jake looked at me and said, "I have the perfect trainer for you. I'll be right back."

I don't know what I expected when Jake returned, but it certainly was not what I got.

Jake walked back toward us and walking behind him was the most gorgeous man I had ever seen. He was tall, chocolatey, and his muscles were so big that my entire face could get lost in his arms.

He stood in front of Mona and me and flashed us the most mesmerizing pearly white smile.

"I want to do training, too. Where do I sign up? I'm ready to write the check," Mona blurted out.

Jake smiled and said to her, "We can take care of that." Then he turned to me. "But first, Ruth, this is Curtis. He's one of our best trainers."

Curtis reached out his hand and grabbed hold of mine. His strong touch made me feel weak at the knees.

"Pleasure to meet you, Ruth." Curtis said.

"Me too, pleasure to meet you. Damn, I need to sign up for personal training," Mona said as she tried jumping in between Curtis and me.

Curtis bit his lower lip trying not to laugh, and that was the sexiest thing I had ever seen.

"Listen, if you got some time now, we can do a few things," Curtis said.

"Oh yeah, absolutely," I said, allowing Curtis to lead me away.

From behind me I could hear Mona yell, "I want to do somethings, Curtis! You know you could at least share, Ruth!"

I could not have been bothered in the least with what Mona was saying. My focus was on this hunk of a man who was directing me into the personal training room.

"Okay, we're going to do a few

exercises so I can see where you are," Curtis said.

I nodded yes, still entranced by how beautiful he was. At that point, he could've said that I needed to leap off the roof of the building and I would've agreed, as long as he would be there to catch me with those strong arms of his.

Curtis took me through a few floor exercises, giving me encouragement along the way. I was so caught up in him that I didn't even realize how much time had gone by, that was until Mona walked in and said, "Um, are you guys going to be all day?"

"We just finished," Curtis replied.

"Oh, already? I was just getting into it," I responded with a flirtatious smile.

"Yes already. Come on let's go; we need to cool your ass off," Mona chimed in.

"Wait, how do I set up another

appointment," I asked Curtis.

"At the front desk, they'll get you set up on a regular schedule," Curtis answered, "until next time, Ruth."

"Yes, absolutely," I said as Mona pulled me out the room.

I couldn't wait for the next time I saw Curtis again. I signed up to work out with him four times a week. It was excessive, but he was just that fine.

Every time we worked out, it was like my body just melted in his hands. His touch was orgasmic and I just wanted more of it. I had never felt this way around a guy before.

"I got to get myself under control," I told Mona.

"Why? You need to just go for it," she would respond.

"What do you want me to do, just jump on him?" I replied.

"Why the hell not? I jumped on that sexy little thing that signed us up, and he was awesome by the way," she said with a smirk.

"You seriously slept with Jake?"

"Sleep had nothing to do with what we did, all night and a little in the morning."

I had to admit that there was something to Mona's level of boldness. I had to do something; my body was literally screaming for this man. I had to find a way to get him out of this gym and all to myself.

Then one day, as if he knew my inner thoughts, Curtis asked, "Hey, do you jog?"

"Nope, I just come here."

"You should. It's the perfect start to your day. How about I stop by your house tomorrow morning and take you for a jog?"

Jackpot! Everything in me wanted to yell out, "Hell yes! Why wait till tomorrow? Let's leave now!"

But the only thing that came out was "okay."

Early that next morning, he came by my house in grey sweatpants and a white t-shirt. He looked too damn good to waste on a jog. I had to go for it. I needed to feel those strong arms around me. I ran my hands along his strong shoulders and leaned in for a kiss. He caught what I was doing and it was on. When he picked me up and lifted me in the air, I was a goner. At that point he could do me however he wanted and did he ever, right there on my living room floor. I was making sounds I never thought I could. My legs went numb and my body shook in ecstasy. The man knew what he was doing.

After that, our relationship was based on working out and having amazing sex. He made my days better. He was the perfect stress reliever. To me everything was good. We weren't serious, but we were solid. We weren't the couple that would go out on dates, but we kept each other's attention very well.

That was until Curtis decided to get a little weird on me. All of a sudden, it seemed like us just hanging out was not good enough and everything I said bothered him. I kept feeling like he was always on edge, always testy. We once got into an argument because I wouldn't spend the night at his place. I didn't understand why all of a sudden it bothered him. I'd never spent the night at his place and he never spent the night at mine; it just wasn't our thing.

Then one day everything just kinda came to a head. Mona opened her art gallery and had this big get together. The guest list was pretty impressive and the art that she was able to collect came from some very talented local artists. I couldn't wait to see how everything came together.

Curtis ended up coming over to my house for a visit just as I was getting ready to walk out the door. He had a look of shock on his face when I said I was headed to the gallery. Not sure if he thought that I should've invited him, after all I didn't see us as being that type of couple.

"Oh, I didn't realize you were going anywhere tonight," he said.

"Yeah, tonight is Mona's gallery opening. Maybe we can catch up later," I replied.

"Well, I don't have anything planned. Why don't I come with you?" Curtis said.

"Oh, you don't have to do that. You'll

probably be bored and you're not really dressed for it," I said to him.

Curtis looked down at his black denim jeans and polo shirt in confusion. He then lifted his head and looked at me in disbelief.

"Oh, okay. I guess I'll see you later," he said and started to walk away.

"I'll call you later," I said as he walked off.

A part of me felt bad. But while Curtis was a great guy, he didn't seem to fit into my world. He was a gym guy, not the type that would be comfortable in an art gallery discussing Cubism or Surrealism. That just wasn't his thing. At least I didn't think it was.

The next day he didn't answer my calls, but he came over later that afternoon. His face was serious and his body language was standoffish. He barely looked at me. When he walked in my house, there was no hello or how are you. He just said, "Ruth, I think we may need to cool it for a while, you know, take a break from whatever it is we're doing."

I was stunned by his words and tone. The peace that usually radiated from him was replaced by hurt and distress. He didn't seem like himself anymore. He didn't seem like the fun guy that I met who made me laugh and brought joy to my days.

"You're breaking up with me?" I asked him.

"I just think we both got other things going on right now," he answered.

"Um, okay, I mean, if that's what you want," I said to him not really sure how to respond or where all of that was coming from.

"Yeah, I think it's best," he said, giving me a kiss on the cheek and then walking out of my house and my life.

I instantly missed him. It was as if I was living in a space where he was the right person who arrived in my life at the wrong time. I never really understood why Curtis wanted to break it off with me. I just never had the nerves to ask him, or maybe I just didn't care enough.

"Why am I here, Ruth?" Curtis asked. There was no real emotion in his face, just confusion. He didn't seem upset but suspicious.

I took a deep breath and looked at him. "I've sorta been taking stock of my life lately."

"Okay, what does that have to do with me?" Curtis asked again.

"Well, what I've been doing is, well . . . why did we break up, Curtis? I mean, why did you feel the need to break up with me?" I watched as he sat back in his chair with an even more confused look on his face. "I mean, it's not like I'm here looking to get back together. I'm just being curious." I tried to sound not as crazy as the whole situation seemed. But the fact was I wouldn't have blamed him at all if he just got up and walked away.

"That's a crazy question to ask after all these years," he said.

"I know it is. But I really need you to be honest with me," I told him.

"Okay, well honestly, it was just a lot of little things," he said.

"What does that mean? I thought we

had fun together," I responded.

"Yeah, we did. But at times it felt like you preferred me at an arm's length. Nothing I did or said seemed good enough. It just became hard to approach you with information. I think that for two people to stay together there should be a comfort level. We just didn't have that."

"I'm not sure I understand what you mean," I said. "Why did you think you couldn't approach me?"

"I don't know. It's just that when two people are in a relationship, a real relationship they should have deep conversations, share their feelings, have some connection."

"I thought we were good."

"Yeah, you probably did, but I wanted more, I guess. I don't think you did."

"I just, I didn't think . . ."

"It's alright, Ruth. I just wasn't the guy you wanted me to be and that's fine," he said with a slight smile. "I guess I just got tired of feeling like there was nothing I could do that would be right."

"Wow, I guess I didn't consider that I was making you feel that way," I said to him.

"Maybe we just wanted two different things from the relationship," he replied.

"I'm sorry," I said, feeling awful and disappointed in myself.

"For what?" he asked.

"For making you feel like you weren't good enough," I answered.

"It's all in the past now, Ruth; life goes on," he said.

"Yeah but . . ." I started to say.

"But nothing. We're both in good places in our lives. It was a lesson," he said with those eyes that smiled at you with peace radiating from them.

It was in that moment when I realized what an amazing person Curtis was. I don't think I had ever gone past his physical appearance to get to the man. Someone who was just meant to be a great distraction could've been so meaningful in my life had I looked deeper, had I given him a chance to show me the type of man he was, had I been willing to see him for the man he was. I guess Curtis came into my life at the wrong time or maybe I just wasn't ready to see past the exterior. I wasn't feeling like he was the one that got away or that we should give it another try; I guess I had just realized that there may be more to someone than what I see.

I sat at the table for a while after Curtis left and watched the endless stream of people as they came in and out of nearby businesses. This one older lady caught my eye. She had a pleasant face as if she knew all the good that filled the world.

I saw her come out of the nearby grocery store pushing her shopping cart. When she stepped onto the side walk, she must have missed a step because she went tumbling and landed on the ground. I jumped up and ran over to her.

"Are you okay?" I asked as I knelt down next to her.

"Oh, I'm fine, just really clumsy," she said with an embarrassed grin.

"Here, let me help you up," I said to

her.

As I helped her off the ground, I noticed that she had a little limp. I guided her to a nearby bench and sat her down. She kept rubbing on her ankle and making a face as if she was in pain.

"Do you need me to do anything for you? Call someone?" I asked.

"My grandson dropped me off earlier and he should be coming back soon. I think I'll just sit here until he gets here," she explained.

"Do you mind if I sit here with you?" I asked. I didn't want to leave her until I was sure she would be alright.

"Of course you can, honey," she said. "What is your name?"

"Ruth, my name is Ruth," I said to her.

"Well, it's a pleasure to meet you, Ruth. I'm Beatrice but folks just call me Grandma

Bee," she said with a smile.

"It's a pleasure to meet you, too, Grandma Bee," I said.

There was something so warm about Grandma Bee. Her smile made you feel like curling up in her arms and letting her sing you to sleep.

"So, tell me about yourself, Ruth? Are you married?" she asked.

"No, I'm not," I answered.

"Dating someone special?" she continued to ask.

"No," I answered with an awkward smile.

"What is a pretty girl like you doing by yourself?" she asked.

That's the question that every single woman of a certain age hates to be asked. It makes you feel like you've failed somewhere along the line. As if you've done something to make yourself undesirable to the entire male species.

But something told me that Grandma Bee didn't mean anything by it. I didn't want to put all my current feelings on her and make her feel uncomfortable so I simply said, "Guess I haven't found the right man yet."

Grandma Bee smiled and tapped me on my knee saying, "He'll come along; you have to keep the faith. When I met my husband, I knew right away he was the one."

"Did you?" I asked with a grin. "How? Was there something special about him?"

"No, he got on my last nerves," Grandma Bee giggled.

"Really?" I grinned.

"Oh Lord, yes. He was just the most annoying thing. Always following me around and paying me compliments. Lord, that man just would not let me be. But I'm glad he didn't because we had an amazing life together with a beautiful daughter that gave us two wonderful grandsons. You know, he once told me that he knew the moment he saw me that I was the one."

"Wow, so then I guess my answer to your previous question is I haven't found a man who knew I was the one," I said.

Grandma Bee let out a loud laugh, "Oh sweetheart, you don't find that kind of man; he finds you and refuses to let you go."

I was so distracted by what Grandma Bee was saying that I didn't notice the man who came up to us and bent over to give Grandma Bee a hug.

"Grandma Bee, is everything okay?" the male voice said.

I looked up and it was Bo. He turned

and smiled at me as if he was glad to see me.

"I'm fine. This beautiful, young single lady took very good care of me," Grandma Bee said.

"Hi Ruth," Bo said as he stood up straight. "Thanks for looking after my grandma."

"Hi Bo. It was not a problem at all; I think she took care of me," I replied with a grin.

"So you two know each other?" Grandma Bee asked.

"Yes, we've met before," I said. "I should be going. It was great meeting you, Grandma Bee."

"It was great meeting you, too, Ruth," Grandma Bee replied.

"Bye Ruth, thanks again," Bo said.

"Bye," I responded with a slight wave

and started to walk away.

"Ruth, don't forget to keep your eyes out," Grandma Bee called out to me.

I turned around and asked, "For what?"

"You'll know it when it finds you," she answered with a smile.

I sat in the swing chair on my back porch as it slowly swung back and forth. The sound of the saxophone tried to soothe my wondering mind as it played every emotion that ran through my body.

Curtis had taken me for a loop. I didn't expect that he would be more than what I thought he was. I had been wrong about Brandon. I had been wrong about Curtis. Now I was even more confused than ever. This whole thing was starting to take a toll on me mentally. I wasn't sure how it was supposed to help me. So far, the only thing I'd discovered about myself was that I let men walk all over me and I didn't make it easy for them to approach me about their true feelings. The only question I have is: how in the hell do I fix that? I didn't hang in there with Curtis and we broke up. I did hang in there with Brandon and we still broke up. So what does all that mean? Am I supposed to ride until the wheels fall off, or should I jump off at the first sign of trouble?

The ringing of the doorbell provided a much needed distraction from the thoughts running, or rather sprinting, through my mind. On the other side of the door were Mona and Gloria. They were ready and eager to hear about what happened with Curtis, especially Mona.

I explained to them everything he said and waited for the girlfriend's soothing verbiage, "Oh girl, he's tripping; that is so not you; he's just looking for an excuse," but that never came.

Instead, Gloria leaned in to me and said, "As much as I think this is the most ridiculous thing ever, he does have a point."

"Gloria!" I yelled out.

"Here me out," she replied. "Look what happened at my house the other night; you didn't want to give Donald a chance. He could have been more but you just heard one thing and you were out. You refused to look beyond the surface."

"It was more than one thing, Gloria," I responded.

"My point is, you could have given him a chance," she said.

"He wasn't my type," I said.

"How did you know that?" she asked. "You never even gave him a chance."

"I know what my type is," I replied.

"Oh, do you?" she asked, giving me a smirk.

I rolled my eyes knowing that she was trying to hint that I had absolutely no clue what my type was but I did, I think.

"Forget all of that," Mona chimed in. "What about the next guy? He could say something completely different."

"Oh no, I think I've had enough. Besides, the guy I dated before Curtis was so cheap. I mean, we're still cool and all but I don't need to find him and find out what went wrong," I told her.

"You mean Ethan? Well if you're interested, I know where he'll be next weekend," Mona said teasingly.

"I think I've had enough," I said.

"Maybe you should. You and Ethan were friends before, so maybe he could really break this all down for you," Gloria said.

"I thought you thought this whole thing was stupid?" I asked Gloria.

"No, I think it's ridiculous, but since you've already started, you might as well see it through," Gloria replied.

I shook my head in disbelief. "Where is he going to be?" I reluctantly asked Mona.

"His friend Greg told me that he's getting married this weekend," Mona replied.

"You want me to go crash this man's wedding to find out why we broke up?" I asked in disbelief.

"Girl no, that would be crazy. I want you to go to the bachelor party the night before," Mona said.

"Okay, so I think this whole thing is stupid, like really stupid," Gloria added.

"I'm not doing that, Mona," I told her.

"Just hear me out," Mona said.

"It better be good," I said.

"Before they go to Greg's house for the 'no girls except strippers allowed' part of the party, they will be at Oasis Nightclub. We can meet them there," Mona said.

"There is absolutely no way that I'm going to a nightclub to ask a man who is about to be married why we're not together. Absolutely no way," I said to Mona, but from the ecstatic look on her face, I knew that I had already lost the argument.

The Eyes of Love

Part 4:

Legacy

The Eyes of Love

Mona and I stood outside Oasis Nightclub waiting for the bouncer to let us in. Mona insisted that she was cool with the DJ, but the bouncer wasn't buying it. I kept telling her that it must be a sign that the universe didn't want us to get into the club. Well it looked like the universe had a change of heart because the bouncer looked at a text message on his phone then he removed the rope and said to us, "Go ahead."

Mona pulled my hand and led me through the doors; if I could've had that spoiled child begging for candy, rolling on the ground screaming tantrum, I would've. Even though Ethan and I were friends before getting involved, showing up to his bachelor party had to be the weirdest shit ever. If he would've thought I had lost my mind, he would've been absolutely right.

"Oh my God, there they are," Mona said exactingly.

She pointed to a group of men in a VIP area that were laughing and tossing their bottles of liquor in the air.

I spotted Ethan in the middle. He looked to be having the time of his life and completely into the fun he and his boys were having.

"Let's go over there," Mona said as she leaned into my ear to make sure I heard her over the loud music.

"No, he's having fun. Let's do this some other time," I replied and turned to leave.

But Mona pulled me by the arm again and led me up to the entrance of the VIP section. Neither Ethan nor anyone of his friends even noticed us. Mona kept swinging her hands encouraging me to go in. But I refused. She grew frustrated and started looking around.

Before I knew it, Mona had pushed me into a waitress who was walking by with a full tray of glasses. The tray fell out of the waitress's hand sending the glasses crashing to the ground. It made such a loud smashing sound that Ethan and his friends turned around to see what was going on.

But I was so busy being mortified and apologizing to the waitress that I didn't even notice that Ethan and some of his friends had walked over to see if we were alright.

"Ruth?" Ethan looked shockingly into my face.

"Hey Ethan," I replied.

"Are you alright?" He asked.

"Yeah, I'm fine. Just lost my footing I guess," I tried to explain while looking over my shoulder at Mona who had a look of pure glee on her face.

"Wow, you look great," he said with a smile.

His words made me blush, remembering all the great times we had together. We were pretty good friends and used to have great conversations. In that moment, I forgot that we were standing in the middle of his bachelor party and all I saw was my friend.

"Ethan, do you mind if we step outside for a moment? I really need to ask you something," I said to him.

He looked back at his friends who had gone back to partying. "Yeah, sure." Ethan gently held the lower of my back and led me outside. It was now or never. I didn't know if Ethan would be understanding or completely flipped out because I was bringing this to him the night before his wedding. But there was no turning back.

As we walked outside, the sound of the music faded in the background and all I could hear was the sound of my heart beating. Once again my nerves were all over the place. I didn't want Ethan to look at me differently or think I was trying to stop his wedding.

As he stood staring at me with a look of confusion covering his face, I knew that I had to say something. I also had to be willing to hear whatever it was that he had to tell me.

Ethan & Ruth

When I first met Ethan, I was at this crazy place in my life. I was at a job that I didn't really like, and I couldn't wait to move out of my small apartment. I would look out my window at work and see all the people walking around with their fancy suits and briefcases and wanted to be just like them.

But it seemed that everything I tried just wasn't working. I remember reading somewhere that everything was about the mind and if you wanted to do something different, then you had to change how you thought. So that's exactly what I did.

In my mind I was already one of those people; no one could tell me different. I started hanging out where they hung out and dressing the way they dressed.

I was ready to live the life I had always dreamt of. The life that I was working so hard to achieve. It was way past time to start my black girl *Sex in the City* life. I wanted it all.

The anxiety of trying to make something out of my life was catching up to me. I had a decent job by most standards, but I wanted more. I worked like a crazy person just trying to get my foot in the door only to find myself standing at the same spot, far from the door.

My only solace of sanity was the weekly game nights. It was the one night a week that I would get together with friends and just have fun. No worries about being an adult and all that came with it. It was also where I met Ethan.

Ethan was a great guy who always had a smile on his face. It seemed like he had real goals for himself. He had just passed the bar and was starting his own practice with some friends. Ethan was solid. I figured I needed a solid guy in my life. We could build a strong life together and we hit it off from the first moment we met. We became immediate Spades partners and basically couldn't be beat.

"Okay, I'm tired of y'all cheating all the time!" Mona yelled out as Ethan and I smiled and gave each other high fives from across the table.

Ethan and I had beaten everyone else and they were all in the living room watching the game. The only team that was left was Mona and her current boyfriend, at least for that night. We were winning so much that we even had our own dance.

Every time we did it, Mona's face would frown up in disgust; I loved it.

After everyone's focus was completely on the football game on T.V., I snuck away into the kitchen to find something to drink. It seemed that the only thing being provided was wine and beer, but I was in the mood for something nonalcoholic. As I was rummaging through the fridge, Ethan snuck up behind me and scared the crap out of me. The sound of me yelling was like laughing gas to him. I playfully smacked him to get him to stop.

"Alright, alright, I'm sorry," he said still softly chuckling. "What are you doing in here anyway?"

"Looking for something to drink," I replied.

"There's a whole lot of stuff to drink out there," he said pointing toward the living room.

"I'm not really in the mood to get drunk tonight."

Ethan shook his head and reached around me, pulling out a small bottle of water. He reached out to hand it to me then quickly jerked it back.

"I'll give you this bottle of water on one condition," he said.

"And what's that?"

"Go out with me."

"What?"

"You heard what I said; you agree to go out with me and this nice thirst quenching bottle of water is all yours."

"Or I could just go back in the fridge and get me another one."

"True, that may work, too," he said with a chuckle, "but then that'll mean we don't get to go out. Now what sense does that make?"

I smiled at Ethan. I had never been one to date friends but everything about Ethan and I just made sense. We both were headed in the same direction in life and ready to take on the world. Why not see if we could take it on together?

"Fine," I said as I grabbed the bottle water from his hand, "but you better be on time picking me up."

Ethan burst out into laughter and replied, "I'll be there thirty minutes late just to see what you'll do."

The next night, Ethan came by to pick me up for our date. It was an amazing first date. We already knew each other, so it was super comfortable. None of that awkward first date stuff, like trying to come up with conversation or trying to get to know what the other person liked; we had plenty to say to each other and I already knew his likes and dislikes. It was just like it always was all the other times we hung out, the only difference was that it was just the two of us.

It was just incredible being with someone who was a friend and someone you could see yourself growing with. We just made sense. Two young up and coming professionals living in a vibrant up and coming professional city. We were meant to do great things together.

It seemed like we were on the same page; we both were at the same stage in life and going in the same direction. All our friends knew each other, and everyone hung out like family. We would talk about goals for ourselves and what we wanted our future to look like. Even the fact that he was a little tight with money didn't bother me because I knew he was building a business. So what if we went to the local Wing Stop for dinner as opposed to the five star restaurant further up the street. I was okay with that because we made sense.

But after a few months or so of dating, it was like we stopped making sense. We just were not on the same page anymore. I would do whatever I could, spend whatever money I had just to get us into different fundraisers or networking events. But all he ever wanted to do was go bowling or play pool with his boys.

"Why would I want to hang around some stuffed shirt people I don't know Ruth?" he would ask. "I'm good right where I am."

"How do you intend on growing a law practice if you don't go out and meet people?" I would ask.

"By being a damn good attorney," he

would respond.

"But these people can help you take your practice to the next level," I would counter.

"I kinda like the level I'm on now; you're the one who seems to have an issue with it," he would respond.

"I don't have a problem with it," I would say.

"You could have fooled me," he would reply.

It started to become painfully obvious that Ethan and I just didn't want the same things after all. The man who I thought had all this ambition and drive was not who Ethan turned out to be. He was good with mediocrity. I wanted more. I wanted to be something, to move up in life and to make my mark. I didn't understand how anyone wouldn't want to be at their best.

I began to realize that his cheapness was his thing. Not a means to an end. Not a save for the future but a just not wanting to spend the money.

We tried to hold on for as long as we could, for the sake of our friendship. But in the end, it just wasn't meant to be.

One day we were sitting on his sofa watching T.V. and we just both looked at each other and knew. Ethan turned to me and asked, "This isn't working is it?"

"No, I don't think it is," I replied.

"So, what do you think we should do?" he continued to ask.

"Walk away as friends?" I said shrugging my shoulders.

Ethan wrapped his arms around me and said, "Always friends."

After that Ethan and I tried to hang around one another, like we used to, but it always seemed a bit awkward. After a while, we just stopped showing up to places and events where we knew the other person would be and pretty soon the friendship was out the window. We had gone years without seeing or speaking to each other . . . until now.

"Ruth, are you okay?" Ethan asked

"Oh yeah, I'm fine," I replied.

"So, what's up?" he asked again.

"Well, this is going to seem really crazy. But I promise you this has nothing to do with you getting married tomorrow or this being the night of your bachelor party. Okay, so maybe it is a little bit crazy. I mean, at the very least it's absolutely bad timing and . . ."

"Ruth, you're babbling," Ethan interrupted. "What is it?"

"Ethan, um, why did we break up?" I asked after taking a deep breath.

"What?" he had a look of confusion.

"I mean, if there was something wrong with me, then I can completely understand. But I really need to know why," I said.

"Wow, that's a little out of left field," he said.

"Yeah, well I told you it would sound crazy," I told him

"Yeah, it does," he said scratching his forehead. "I mean, why are you asking me this?"

"I'm just trying to figure somethings out, you know take stock of my life. I just really need to know," I said.

"I mean, we just didn't fit. We both agreed to that," he replied.

"It has to be deeper than that, Ethan. You pulled away from me long before we decided to call it off. Just be honest; I can take it," I said not sure if I could take it at all.

"Ok, honestly?" he asked.

"Yeah, honestly," I answered.

"Well, you were a bit high maintenance for my liking. You always wanted to go to fancy places and have fancy things. To me, just hanging out together was good enough," he explained.

"Wait, what?" I asked. Ethan's response came out of nowhere. "It wasn't about having fancy things or going to fancy places. It was about building a life. I was just trying to put us in front of people that could help us grow."

"Well, I kinda felt like I was doing alright. Those things just were not for me, those people were not my people. I was just trying to build my practice and be content; you wanted to be with the folks at the top. I couldn't give you what you wanted, and I wasn't going to stop being me just so you could live in some fantasy world," he explained.

All of a sudden it felt like Ethan and I were in two different relationships. I thought we were building and he thought I was being greedy.

"Wow, that was not what I expected," I told him.

"Don't take it in a bad way, Ruth," Ethan said.

"Really? Because you just said I was materialistic. How should I take it?" I asked him, feeling myself getting a bit upset.

"You should take it that people want what they want and there's nothing wrong with that," he said.

"Alright E, this club is dead. Time for part two!" a male voice yelled from behind me.

Ethan looked over my shoulder and nodded his head signaling that he was on his way. He then looked back over at me.

"Listen, I've got to go," he said to me. "Are you going to be okay?"

"Yeah, I'll be fine. Go have fun and congratulations, Ethan," I said to him. But I didn't know if I was okay. I never thought of myself as materialistic. I just wanted to be successful and to have something to show for that success.

Ethan smiled at me and walked away. Mona came up and held my hand.

"Are you cool, Ruth?" she asked.

"Nope," I replied. "Let's just go."

When Mona dropped me off at home, it

was almost one in the morning and my street was like a ghost town. I stepped out of Mona's car and began walking toward my front door feeling like I had no clue who I was and wanting so desperately to get myself back.

"Ruth, do you want me to come in?" Mona yelled from her car. "We could have some wine and talk about how crazy men are, you know, make it a girls' night."

"No, I just want to go to bed," I replied.

"Okay, call me tomorrow and let me know you're alright," Mona said before driving off.

I kicked off my shoes as soon as I entered the house. At first I sat quietly in the pitch dark but then I got up to get something to drink. I turned on the light in my kitchen and opened my refrigerator. I don't know when or how it started, but tears began to flow from my eyes. The more I wiped them away, the more they came running down. I almost lost the feeling in my legs and dropped to the floor when the saxophone began to play. It echoed through the streets, bouncing on the pavement and landing effortlessly in my ears. The sound drowned out every thought, and for a moment, I felt like me again.

I spent almost the entire weekend locked away in my house. I didn't want to talk to anyone. My only company was the saxophone that often played from the house next door. I guess I just needed time to think, to process all this new information I had learned about myself.

In some ways I felt incomplete, like

there were still aspects of myself, of my life, that were still a mystery to me. That was such a funny feeling because for so long I thought I was on the right track. That the only part of my life that was lacking was my love life. I never considered that my love life was lacking because I was lacking.

That was a tough pill to swallow. I thought my life was in order; I thought I was in order. But I guess it was all a lie. I was just lying to myself, convincing myself that the problems in my love life existed because I hadn't found the right guy. But the truth was, I found a couple of right guys; I just wasn't the right girl.

After sulking all day and all night, I noticed that Mona had texted me, telling me that she would be at her studio and to come by or call or send out a smoke signal letting her know I was alright. Because I was driving myself crazy in the house, I decided to throw on some yoga pants and a sweatshirt and go to Mona's studio.

When I got there, she was nowhere to be found. There was actually no one there, except Bo. He was so busy nailing and hammering away that he didn't hear me come in. I yelled out, "Hello," but he still didn't hear me. I walked closer to him and yelled again, "Hello!"

He stopped and turned toward me as if I had startled him. "Oh, hey Ruth. How are you?" he said as he stood up straight to face me.

"I'm fine. Is Mona around?" I asked him.

"She was, but I think she may be up in her apartment," he replied.

"Oh, okay. Sorry for bothering you; I'll

let you get back to your work," I said to him.

"Wait, can you help me with something?" he asked.

"Um, okay. What do you need?" I responded.

"I just need you to hold something in place for me," he said.

"What?" I asked.

"This board." Bo tapped his toe on a wood board that laid on the floor. Then he knelt down and looked up at me. He raised his hand to help me get down and showed me how to hold the board in place.

I looked at Bo and asked, "Why are you here working all by yourself? Where's your crew of teens?"

Bo let out a chuckle and answered, "It's Sunday. They deserve the day off."

"Why do you only have teens working

for you?" I continued to ask.

"Do you know a better way to keep them off the streets?" he responded with a smile.

"Oh, so this and the car wash are like charity work?" I asked.

"No. They are both my businesses and I hire and pay young people who want to learn the value of hard work," he answered.

"So they don't already know the value of hard work?" I asked again.

"Did you when you were that age?" Bo asked with a smile. "Sometimes we just need to be reminded of our value. We need to understand that we're good, just the way we are, and we know that because of the people around us who care about what happens to us."

"Why does it feel like you're not talking about your workers anymore?" I looked at him and noticed he had an expression on his face as if he knew something that I didn't.

"Well, Mona said that you may be a little upset with her," he said.

"No, I'm not. Oh my God, she didn't tell you anything else did she?" I was mortified that Mona may have explained my entire situation to him.

"No. I could just tell that she was worried about you," he said.

"Well I'm fine," I said standing up and feeling like I needed to put as much space between me and Bo as possible. "Are we done? Because I have to get going."

"Yeah, we're done. Thank you, Ruth," Bo said.

I awkwardly waved bye and made my way upstairs to Mona's apartment. Mona opened the door on the first knock and flung her arms around me.

"Oh my God, Ruth! Are you okay? Come in," she ushered me into her apartment with joyful glee. It was as if she hadn't seen me in years.

"I'm fine," I said as I sat down on her sofa.

"Are you sure? Because you didn't answer any of my calls or texts. Gloria said to back off and give you time but seeing as how this whole thing was my idea, I just wanted to make sure you weren't at home slitting your wrist or something," Mona said.

"Slitting my wrist is a bit extreme, but Gloria was right. I just needed some time," I replied.

"Are you okay now?" Mona continued to ask.

"I think so," I replied.

"Ethan must have said something crazy left field and I'm sorry. Had I known I never would have pushed the issue," she said.

"He said I was materialistic," I told her.

"That's it?" she asked.

"What do you mean 'that's it?'" I turned to look at her in shock.

"Well, you kinda are, Ruth," she said.

"What!" I yelled out.

"Okay, hear me out. You want what you want and there's nothing wrong with that. There's nothing wrong with wanting more," she explained.

"Apparently there is, at least for Ethan anyway," I told her.

"Then that's his lost. I mean, I wouldn't define you as materialistic, just driven and any guy that's not willing to see that fire in you isn't deserving of you," she said.

"Thank you, I guess," I sat back on the sofa and folded my arms.

Mona mimicked me and then asked, "So is this the end of it?"

"I want to scream yes, but I want to see this through. I want to be able to say that this whole mess has left me changed. But I can't right now. I still have a lot of questions," I explained.

"I was so hoping you'll say that," Mona jumped up with excitement. "So, who's next?"

"Nope, I'm not going to tell you that," I said as I got up and walked toward the door.

"Oh come on, Ruth, let me make up for Ethan," Mona responded as she followed me.

"Maybe next time. Things were a bit weird with this guy and I think I need to approach him on my own," I said.

"Okay, but call me if you need me," she said.

"I will," I replied.

Part 5:

Don't Let Your Past Hold You

For the first time since I started this whole thing, it felt like my nervousness had eased up a bit. I didn't feel like I was this crazy person chasing after the ghost of boyfriends past. It started to feel like I was supposed to learn something; I just wasn't sure what that something was. There was really nothing else I could hear about myself that would shock me anymore. I'd heard it all by that point, I think. But what was the lesson? Not to be a doormat? Check. To look below the surface when it comes to guys? Check. Not to be materialistic, even though I didn't think I was? Check.

So what was next? What else was there

for me to hear? I sat at the table and looked out the window into the distance of the night. The noise of the full restaurant did nothing to break my concentration. For the first time I was focused. Clearly everything I thought I knew about myself was just not true. I needed to finish seeing myself through the eyes of others. For them to tell me how to become whole. It turned out that Mona's stupid idea was actually doing some good.

"Hey girl," Gloria said as she sat down across from me. "Sorry I'm late. Did you order yet?"

I know I told Mona that I wanted to do this one on my own but I really wanted someone objective by my side, and no one is more objective than Gloria. I needed her rational thinking to help me put everything in perspective.

"No, not yet. I was waiting on you," I replied.

"Okay good, I'm starving," she responded.

The waiter came over and we placed our orders. I looked around the restaurant, glancing at every face that passed me. None of them were him. A friend of a friend told me that I would find him here but that didn't seem to be the case.

"Are you alright?" Gloria asked.

"Yeah," I replied.

"Okay, so what's the game plan?" Gloria asked again.

"Not sure. I don't see him," I answered.

"Are you sure he's here?" Gloria continued.

"Yeah, I think," I said.

I called the waiter over and asked him, "What's the name of your sous-chef?"

"Edward and William and I think there's a new chick," he said.

"No. Well is there a Marcus?" I asked.

"The only Marcus is the owner and the head chef," he replied.

"Oh, so you have a Marcus who's the owner and a Marcus who's the head chef?" I asked.

"No. The owner Marcus is the head chef," he answered.

I looked around the restaurant not having realized how well Marcus had done for himself. I always had known that he wanted to be a chef but didn't think he would actually own a restaurant. When we were together, he was studying to be chef and working as a bartender.

"Is it possible for me to speak with him?" I asked the waiter.

"Yeah, I guess. I'll go find him in the

back," the waiter replied.

"Thank you so much. Ruth! Please tell him Ruth is here to see him," I said catching myself in mid shout.

When he walked away, Gloria stared at me while eating her salad. I could almost hear what she was thinking but was not ready to acknowledge it. I turned my head from her and took a sip of my wine. As I looked out the window, I could see the shadow of a man in a white chef's coat walking up behind me.

I turned to see a caramel tone, tall, masculine man with a neatly sculpted beard. Marcus was just as I remembered him. He always had an air of confidence and assurance that surrounded him. Marcus always knew who he was and what he wanted. I had always admired that about him. Although we never really got serious, I always wondered about him from time to time. He was a decent guy. I just think we both were not ready to take things to the next level. He was focused on school and I was just getting out of school and out of a serious relationship. I think the timing was off for us.

"Wow, Ruth. It's been a long time," he said as I got up to give him a hug.

He hugged me and then Gloria, greeting us both warmly. He acted as if no time had gone by as he chatted about his restaurant with Gloria and me. The base in his voice danced with joy with each explanation of how he brought his dream to life. I found myself being very impressed with him. Marcus always had been the kind of guy that girls would deem to be husband material. He was one of the good ones.

Marcus & Ruth

I was fresh out of college and ready for the world. The problem was it didn't seem as if the world was ready for me. I had just broken up with my college boyfriend; we had been together since freshman year and he was my best friend. My heart was in a million pieces. Then to make it worse, I couldn't find a decent job to save my life.

I had applied to about a hundred different positions and only seemed to get two interviews. After one of those interviews, which went absolutely nowhere, I found myself in need of a drink. I walked into a bar in the art district and there he was behind the bar, serving drinks and smiling as if he didn't have a care in the world.

I was instantly attracted to Marcus, but in that moment there was so much going wrong in my life that I couldn't work up the effort it would take to flirt and get his attention. Luckily, I didn't have to. As soon as I sat down at the bar, he came over and poured me a glass of wine.

"You look like you need this," he said with a smile.

"Thank you. I do," I replied.

"You want to talk about it?" he asked.

"I don't think I'm okay with telling my business to a stranger," I responded.

"Well I'm Marcus and if you tell me your name, we won't be strangers," he said as he gave me the sexiest grin he could muster.

"I'm Ruth, but I still don't feel like sharing," I said to him.

"Are you sure about that?" he asked.

"To me, it always seems easier to share with someone you don't know."

I looked at the genuine kindness on Marcus's face and opened up to him. I told him about my break up and about not being able to find a job and about my crazy roommate Mona. He was actually right; it felt good to talk to someone that I didn't know. There was no judgement, just a listening ear.

When I was done, he poured me another glass of wine and said, "It seems to me that you're not that bad off."

"Are you serious? Did you hear everything I just said?" I asked him.

"I heard every word you just said," he replied.

"And you think I'm not that bad off?" I asked again.

"I do," he answered.

"Please explain," I said with a disbelieving chuckle.

"Well, everyone getting out of college can't find a job so you're pretty much in good company. Your roommate may be a pain but she seems to really care about you because she's letting you stay there rent free and had you not broken up with your boyfriend, you wouldn't be free to go out with me," he told me.

I had to laugh. But it wasn't one of those this guy is insane laughs; it was one of those blushing, "he likes me" type of laughs. I was flattered. He was charming and caring and said all the right things. What else could I do but agree to go out with him?

Marcus was an attentive boyfriend. He'd always listen as I talked, he knew what I liked without me saying anything,

174

and he always found ways to make my day better. I liked having him around. I appreciated his effort.

"Okay, close your eyes," Marcus instructed as he came to into the bedroom on one of those nights that I couldn't fall asleep.

"Why?" I asked curious as to what he was up to.

"Just close your eyes," he said again.

I obliged and waited for him to do whatever it was he was going to do.

"Open your eyes," he whispered as he sat on the edge of the bed next to me.

When I did, he handed me a mug of steaming hot chocolate filled with marshmallows. I couldn't help but smile. Life had been kicking my ass lately and the fact that Marcus thought that it could all be fixed with some hot chocolate made my heart smile.

"Take a sip," Marcus said through a sexy grin.

I sipped the hot chocolate and it was the best thing ever. "Oh my God, this is so good. What's in it?"

"My special recipe," he replied.

"So you can cook *and* make fantastic hot chocolate?"

"Well you know, I do what I can," he winked. Then he lied down on the bed next to me and continued, "How about I hold you until you fall asleep?"

"That would be nice."

I set my mug down and lied on Marcus's chest. I felt comfortable and safe. I knew that all Marcus wanted to do was take care of me. But for some reason it was just so hard for me to let him.

There was so much that my heart was

missing, but I couldn't put it into words what it was. I loved being around Marcus and I loved having him in my life. He was this positive force in my life at a time I really needed it. But I thought it should've been more. I wanted it to resemble the relationship that I had before him, but it just didn't feel the same. One day I sat in the middle of my living room floor going through old photos and letters. My ex used to write a lot; he would write me poems and short notes to encourage me and remind me that he loved me.

Maybe that's what I was missing, a little encouragement. Just a reminder that everything was going to work out. Marcus was a great guy, but he was out here chasing his dreams just like me and it's kind of hard encouraging someone when you need encouraging yourself.

I just had so much doubt and my ex was always able to make me feel like I could conquer the world. I stared at a picture of the two of us and my mind wandered. I was so far gone into what was going on the day that photo was taken that I didn't hear Marcus walk in.

He stood behind me, I'm not sure for how long, and didn't say anything. It wasn't until I heard the floor creek that I turned around to see him. His face looked distant and disappointed. He lowered his head and said, "I didn't mean to bother you but I knocked; you didn't answer."

"Oh, sorry. You're not bothering me," I replied as I quickly tried to put away all the photos and letters.

I didn't know if I should explain to Marcus what I had been feeling or if I should just leave it alone. I decided to just leave it alone. He was dealing with his own issues and didn't need me to add mine on top of it. He was focused on finishing culinary school and someday opening his own restaurant. I wanted that for him. I didn't want what I was feeling to be a distraction for him. He deserved everything he was working toward.

Maybe I expected Marcus to just know what to do. My ex always knew, but Marcus just didn't. He was a great guy but there was just something holding us both back, something not quite right between us. I wanted our relationship to be smooth, no issues. For us to know each other inside and out. But we didn't. At times it was like we were just hanging out, keeping each other company for the time being.

One day we went out for a walk through the park, something we did routinely to get some alone time, maybe to connect in a way. Marcus held my hand as we walked. There was an awkward silence. It seemed that we both were feeling something but didn't want to vocalize it. Then Marcus stopped walking and turned to me.

"I think we need to talk, you know, about us," he said.

"Yeah sure," I replied as I sat on a bench that was behind me.

Marcus sat down beside me and continued to hold my hand. He looked at me softly and said, "I really care about you, Ruth, but I'm not sure if we're ready for this."

"You mean for a relationship?" I asked.

"Yeah, I think there's a lot going on with us," he answered.

Even though it sounded like Marcus was trying to let me down easy, I couldn't help but agree with him. There was a lot going on with us, with me.

"Maybe it's just not the right time," I said to him.

"Maybe," he replied. "Hopefully, one day it will be."

"Hopefully," I gave Marcus a smile and that was the last time I saw him.

Here he was, still coated in peace and confidence. Talking like no time had passed between us.

"Wow, you look great, Ruth," he said to me. "It's been a long time."

"Yeah, it has," I replied.

"So, what have you been up to?" he asked me.

I told him all about my job and buying

my first home. He listened intently as always. After I was done talking, he said, "I knew you could do it. I'm proud of you, Ruth."

I smiled knowing that Marcus had always encouraged me and willed me to do more.

"Thank you," I replied. "But look at you, this place is incredible."

"Yes, it's lovely," Gloria said. "But where's the restroom?"

"Straight back that way," Marcus said pointing to a hallway behind him.

Gloria excused herself from the table and walked behind Marcus, throwing me a sign to hurry up and tell him why I was there.

I gave Marcus a shy smile and said to him, "I know me being here seems weird."

"Not really, I always hoped I'd run into

you at some point, just to see how you were doing," he replied.

"Wow, I always thought you were a great guy," I said.

"Thank you, you're not so bad yourself," he said. "But why are you here?"

"Well, I've been sorta going through this crazy stage in my life. I feel the need to find out from guys I've dated why we didn't work out," I shrugged my shoulders with nervous anticipation.

Marcus sat back in his chair and folded his arms. I wasn't sure what he was thinking. He looked far off into the distance as if he was weighing his words carefully. For some reason his silence scared me. It almost seemed like he was going to be like all the rest and tell me something that I wasn't expecting. Some new information about myself.

"That I didn't expect," he said.

"Sorry, I don't mean to come at you with this, not out the blue anyway," I responded.

"No, it's fine. I don't think I said everything I should have back then anyway," he said.

"Everything like what?" I asked.

"Well, like, I felt that there was something between us, something holding us back," he said leaning in and folding his hands on the table.

"I felt that, too," I replied.

"I think what happened with us was that, we were just not able to connect emotionally or spiritually. It's hard to build a relationship when two people are just going through the motions of being in a relationship," he explained.

"That too," I said not surprised by what

he was saying. "So, what do you think it was? Why weren't we ready to be in a relationship?"

"One of us was not, at least not in that relationship," he said.

"What do you mean?" I asked

"I think we started too soon after you ended one relationship. I don't think you were ready to put your heart out there again. Something in you still wanted to be with him," he explained.

I sat back in my chair taking in all that Marcus was saying. I never thought that I was still hung up on my ex. It wasn't like we ended badly; we just grew up and wanted different things. But I liked the comfort and realness of our relationship. At the time I was dating Marcus, I guess I needed that, more than I thought I did. Marcus was the romantic, hold me in the middle of the night until I fell asleep type of guy, but I really wanted the cheering for me on the sidelines type of guy.

"Sorry for bringing that into what we had. But I don't think I wanted him; I just wanted what we had. I thought that's what a relationship should look like," I said to him.

"You don't need to apologize," Marcus replied.

"I've been apologizing a lot lately," I said with a chuckle.

"Well stop. Life happens as it should," he said. "After we broke up, I thought I needed to put relationships on hold for a while, then I found my girl and she was everything I ever imagined the love of my life would be like."

"I'm happy for you, Marcus; you deserved that," I told him.

"Thanks Ruth," He responded. "Listen,

I have to get back in the kitchen, but you come back anytime; you'll always have a table here."

I gave Marcus a smile and waved bye. Unlike the last couple of times I talked to my exes, I didn't feel bad or empty. A big part of me really regretted not having things work out better with Marcus. The today me would've been all over him. But I guess it was one of those things that wasn't meant to be.

"So, what happened?" Gloria asked as she came back to the table and sat down.

"Just bad timing for us," I answered.

"Maybe now is the right timing," Gloria said, giving me a nudge and a smile.

"I think his girlfriend would have something to say about that," I said while pointing to where Marcus was standing. He had his arms around an incredibly beautiful, statuesque woman who laid her head on his shoulder.

"She is gorgeous," Gloria said. "He always had good taste."

Gloria grabbed hold of my hand and gave me a wink. I was happy that an amazing guy like Marcus had found someone who truly loved him and was willing to share her world with him. But I was sad that the same hadn't happened for me.

After we left the restaurant, I went home and thought about everything, not just Marcus but Brandon and Curtis and Ethan. I thought about who I was when I was with each of them and how it all seemed like I was an entirely different woman. The thoughts that were racing through my head started to create a pain in my neck. I started rubbing my neck while I stood in the doorway of my back door. Then, like as if on cue, the saxophone began to play. The sound of it was like a gentle hand that rubbed away every ache in my neck and left me soothed and at peace.

It was a beautiful Sunday morning and I found myself in need of a serious car wash. Bo and his band of teens had done a great job last time, but I really didn't want to run into him again. It felt like, after Mona told him all my business, he looked at me differently. Like I was this crazy, dumb girl who he should feel sorry for. The last thing I needed was someone, some guy, that I didn't know feeling sorry for me.

I sat in my car outside his car wash until I was sure he wasn't there. Then I drove up and asked to have my car taken care of. One young man came up to me. He was covered in tattoos with a head full of dreads. He wouldn't be someone I would feel safe around in a dark alley, but he was really polite and seemed to take pride in his work.

I had to ask him how long he'd been working for Bo. My curiosity about him hiring all these teens had gotten to me and I needed to know more.

"About two years," he said. "Ever since I got out of juvie."

"He hired you after you go out of jail?" I asked. "Why? I mean, not that you didn't deserve a second chance or anything. Because you do, but I just . . ."

"It's okay. Yeah, he did. He actually came and picked me up when I got out. He said he was starting this car wash business and asked me to be part of it," he explained.

"Wow, that's incredible. How do the two of you even know each other?" I asked.

"We didn't; I knew his brother," he said.

"Oh, does his brother work here, too?" I asked.

"Nah, he died," he said. "He was one of my best friends. We got involved in some stupid stuff and it cost him his life. I got busted and was locked up. Bo hated me at first but then something changed, I guess, because he showed up and changed my life."

I looked at the young man and then around at all the young men at the car wash. They were all the same; they were different ages and colors but all the same. All young men who could be out in the streets, all young men who you wouldn't want to meet

J.E. Smythe

in a dark alley, yet here they were, working hard.

I felt a little impressed with Bo in that moment. He was helping them be better people. That's something I had to respect.

After my car was washed, I went to Mona's studio to fill her in on all that had happened with Marcus. But first, I stopped in the coffee shop next door. Sitting there looking through his phone was Bo. I placed my coffee order and then went over to him.

"Good morning," I said.

He looked up and greeted me with a smile, "Good morning to you as well. Please sit down."

"Sure, I can't stay long. I'm on my way to see Mona, as always," I said with a shy smile.

He looked at me as if he was reading my mind. The crazy thing was, I didn't feel uncomfortable or uneasy. He was focused on me and I let him be.

"How are you doing?" he asked.

"I'm good," I replied.

"Listen, about the other day, I didn't mean to overstep," he said.

"No, don't worry about it. I've been on edge lately," I said. "Um, I just came from your car wash and talked to this young man who said you gave him a job when he got out of jail?"

"You have to be specific, a lot of my boys started working for me straight out of jail. Some I got before they went to jail," he said.

"A lot of tattoos, dreads," I described.

"Oh, Andre," he said.

"Yeah, he told me about your brother. I'm sorry for your loss," I responded.

"Thank you," he said. For the first time

since I had met him, he seemed uneasy, like there was something weighing on him. His heart was heavy.

"May I ask how you got through it? Was it working with all those young people?" I asked him.

"Yeah, I think so. I think I felt like I should have done more to help protect my brother. But what I've learned is you can't change the past; you just have to move forward with the lessons learned from it," he explained.

"I just recently learned the dangers of holding on to the past. I'm glad you found something to help you heal, Bo," I said to him.

The barista called my name and I got my coffee and left, waving goodbye to Bo, realizing he had more going for him than I had given him credit for.

Mona was looking at paint colors when I walked in. She immediately burst out, "Gloria already filled me in. I always liked Marcus. You think he and his girlfriend are a permanent thing? Because he may still be carrying a torch for you."

"I think he and his girlfriend are solid. Besides, I don't know if Marcus was the one, not for me anyway," I said.

"Then who was the one?" she asked.

Just then Gloria walked in and said, "I knew the two of you would be here."

She came over and sat down taking my cup of coffee and drinking it.

"Hey!" I shouted out.

"Girl, I need this," she replied.

"How did you know I didn't need it?" I

asked.

"Do you have a husband and two kids? Exactly," she asked and answered her own question. "So what did I miss?"

"Ruth was saying how Marcus was not the one," Mona explained.

"Well of course he wasn't the one," Gloria said. "If he was the one, then you guys would still be together."

"So what's the next game plan?" Mona asked.

"Well, I have one more guy to go," I said.

"Oh my God, the one who was supposed to be the one," Mona responded.

"That's going to be the hardest one, Ruth." Gloria said.

"I know," I replied.

"I'm definitely coming this time and I'm not taking no for an answer," Mona said.

"Um, you do know what he does for a living and where we need to go to meet him, right?" Gloria and I looked at each other with a smirk, knowing that Mona was about to regret volunteering to come with me.

Part 6:

Redemption

The Eyes of Love

The church was packed and filled with an intense energy of joy. People smiled as we walked in and greeted us as if we were family. Mona, in her miniskirt was visibly uncomfortable. I couldn't help but laugh at her. Church was out of her element, far out of her element. She kept tugging at her skirt as if it would suddenly stretch to below her knees and fixing her top to try and hide her peaking cleavage.

"Will you relax? God's not going to strike you down for walking in here," I told her.

"You wouldn't say that if you knew what my night was like last night," she said.

"What exactly was your night like last

night?" I asked her.

"You don't want to know," she answered.

"What did you do last night?" I asked not sure if I was ready for the answer.

"It's not a what as it's more of a who," she said. "Just a one night thing, maybe. You think it would be considered a sin that I can't remember his last name."

"Oh my God, Mona," I said shaking my head.

The choir began singing and everyone stood up and began to clap and sing along. I stood up and Mona looked around noticing that she was the only one still sitting. She reluctantly got up and awkwardly clapped along.

Then I looked up on the altar and there he was, Randel, Pastor Randel. He hadn't changed a bit since the last time I saw him.

It was the night after our college graduation when we decided to part ways. We both felt like it was the right move for us but it took me years to stop loving him, to stop being in love with him.

Randel started preaching and it was like every word had meaning and substance. People hung on to his every word as if they needed him to free them in some way. Some clapped, some smiled and some cried. But they all cherished him for being there. I knew the feeling. It was how I felt about him all those years ago. Seeing him up there brought back all those memories and feelings.

When the service was over, I sat in the back pew and waited for everyone to finish talking to Randel. Mona ran out of the church before the last Amen could be said and told me she'd meet me in the car.

Randel caught a glimpse of me sitting in the back of the church. He ran over to me and almost picked me up off the bench and off my feet. His excitement to seeing me filled me with joy. I had forgotten how good it felt to be in his arms. How he comforted my soul with just one touch.

"Wow, you look great, Ruthie," he said as he put me down. "How have you been?"

"I've been good. It's great to see you, Randel," I replied with a smile.

"It's great to see you, too," he replied. "Here, have a seat."

Randel sat down next to me and placed his arm across the back of the pew behind me. Randel's face was practically glowing and I was nostalgic looking into his eyes. At one point in my life, Randel was my everything. He was the only person that mattered to me. I hadn't realized how much

I missed Randel until that very moment. I was fighting back the urge to grab hold of him and never let him go again. I still remember loving him with everything that was in me.

Randel & Ruth

College was the best time of my life. I had a ball. That first day, freshman year, was the start of it all. It was the day I met my college roommate Gloria and her insane cousin Mona. It was the day I met Randel and he became my world. I still remember that day. Mona, Gloria and Gloria's boyfriend Charlie, who she brought with her, and I were walking in the quad when we saw a group of guys. In the middle of them was this tall, skinny guy who had a smile that lit up everything around him. He immediately caught my eye.

I tried not to look at him, but I just couldn't help myself; he was magnetic. Later that day I went to register for class and there he was with that same smile. Randel walked up to me and I thought my heart was going to melt. He looked at my registration form and said, "Hey, it looks like we have a few of the same classes."

I looked back at his registration form and replied, "Yeah, I guess we do." I looked away from him because it felt like the butterflies in my stomach were going to fly out through my mouth if I said another word.

"Well then, I guess I should introduce myself," he said reaching around me to stretch out his hand. "Hi, I'm Randel."

I turned my head and let my hand meet his. "I'm Ruth."

"Nice to meet you, Ruth," he said while his hand lingered in mine.

I was a goner. After that, Randel and I were inseparable. We spent every waking hour together and some sleeping hours, too. He was the source of all my laughter and made my bad days great. I just knew that Randel and I would be together for a lifetime.

"Come on, Ruthie, you got this," Randel said to me as I was about to give up on studying for my American Lit midterms.

"I don't have any idea about the meaning behind all of this," I said to him.

"What's to know?" he said. "Most of this old stuff is more about feeling and less about reading. You got to start learning to read with your heart, Ruthie; you're always in your head. It's a beautiful head, but your heart isn't so bad either."

I gave Randel a guess and continued studying, as he watched me to make sure I didn't try to give up again. The next day I aced my midterms and the first person I wanted to tell was Randel.

"I knew you could do it, Ruthie," he said scooping me in his arms and holding me tight.

I didn't want Randel to let me go. I felt my strongest when I was in his arms. I knew that no matter what came up, we could face it together. We would sit for hours and talk about our futures; at least he'd listen to me as I ran on for hours about all the plans I had for myself, plans for us.

"That's a whole lot of thoughts running through that head of yours, Ruthie," he would say.

"Yes, but it's all possible and that's all that matters," I replied.

Our future together seemed so real to me. Like it was destined, like we were destined.

But during the summer leading into our last year of college, Randel got into a car accident. I dropped everything to be by his side. Fortunately, he wasn't badly hurt; he had a few bruised ribs and a broken leg. His car was destroyed but he walked away, and I was grateful.

However, something changed in Randel after that. He wasn't the same person. Randel started talking about how God had saved him, and he felt like he was meant for something more than what he was doing or what he had planned on doing. At first, I chalked it up to the side effects of almost losing his life. I thought that he would eventually shake it off, but he didn't.

When I went to parties at night, he stayed home reading the Bible. On Sunday mornings he insisted that I wake up to go to church with him. He wanted us to get more involved in the church to do more volunteer work and help the needy. I believed in God, but it all became too much for me. My life was not heading down the road of saving the world; I wanted to be young and have fun.

A couple of days before graduation, Randel came to my dorm room and said to me that he'd made a decision about his life. I had no idea where he was going, but the serious look on his face scared me. I started to get the feeling that the decision didn't include me.

"What is it?" I nervously asked him.

He sat me down and said, "I've decided

to go into the seminary."

"The seminary?" I asked, confused.

"Yeah, I want to be a priest," he replied.

"What?" My head was spinning. I didn't know what to say or how to act.

"It's my calling, Ruth," he said. "I can make a difference in this world. I can help lead people to the goodness of the Lord."

"Okay, so, what does that mean for us?" I asked. "We had a plan."

"I know, but I have to be true to what God created me to be and as for us, well, I don't know. I don't want to make you live a life you're not comfortable with. I want you to live the life you want," he explained.

"But I want to live my life with you," I told him with tears in my eyes.

"I know, and I want to live my life with you, too, but my choice of how to live that life is not yours and all I want is for you to be happy, Ruth, even if it's not with me," Randel said wiping the tears from my eyes.

"So, this means we're breaking up?" I asked as my heart broke into a million pieces.

"I'm so sorry, Ruth." Randel kissed my forehead and his tears landed on the top of my head.

My whole body went numb as Randel walked out of my dorm room. The vision of my future that had made a permanent home in the back of my mind had gone completely dark and nothing made sense to me anymore.

I had never felt that type of pain before. I hated him but loved him all at the same time. On graduation day, Randel and I went our separate ways and life, especially my love life, never made sense again.

"Man, it's so good to see you," he said as he stared at me.

"Same here," I replied. "You looked amazing up there."

I'd never come to see Randel preach. I guess I was so upset with him that I couldn't bring myself to share this important part of him. But seeing him up on that pulpit reassured me that he was right; that was his calling.

"Thank you," he replied. "So, what brings you here? Not that I'm not happy you came."

"Well, you were my last stop," I said.

Randel let out a loud chuckle, "That was cryptic."

"I know, sorry," I giggled. "I'm just

trying to figure some things out about myself."

"Some things like what?" he asked me.

"Some things like why I don't seem to be the one for anyone," I answered.

Randel started to move in his seat, visibly uncomfortable.

"I'm not losing my mind or trying to give out some type of guilt trip. I'm just trying to figure me out," I said to him, trying to provide him some comfort.

"Wow, Ruthie, that could be a loaded question," he said.

"I know, believe me," I responded. "So..."

"So, what?" he asked.

"So, why wasn't I your one?" I turned my entire body to face him. I didn't want to hear his words only; I wanted to see his face. I wanted him to look me in my face and tell me why we ended, why we couldn't figure out a way to make our lives fit.

"That was a long time ago, Ruthie," he said.

"I know, but I still want to know," I said to him.

"Well my faith became important to me," he said.

"More important than me?" I asked.

"It wasn't about a competition," he said. "Believe me, if I thought I could have both, I would."

"So then you did choose your religion over me?" I asked again.

"No, I chose you," he answered. "I chose your happiness."

"What? I don't understand; how did you choose my happiness?" I continued to ask.

Randel grabbed hold of my hand and squeezed it tightly. Then I saw his eyes.

Sincerity filled them as he said, "You wouldn't have been happy as the wife of a pastor, Ruthie. Living my dreams would have drowned you."

"Or just being with you would have been enough," I said feeling the tears as they began to build. I fought hard to keep them back because I didn't want Randel to think I was still in love with him. The truth was I didn't realize until that moment how much I was still hurting from our breakup.

"You know, I think love is a funny thing. There are loves that last a lifetime and then there are loves that last for a moment in time. We had an amazing moment and I wouldn't have changed it for the world, but our love was not meant to last a lifetime," he explained. "I think a part of you knows that."

"I know, I do, I just . . ." I started to say

before Randel stopped me.

"You said I was the last stop. What did you come away with from the other stops?" he asked.

"Oh, I'm one hell of a girlfriend," I said with a sarcastic smile.

"What does that mean, Ruth?" Randel asked with a chuckle.

"Well apparently, I let men walk all over me, I'm materialistic, I'm not approachable, and I hold on to my past. Oh, and as you pointed out, I'm a heathen. Basically, I'm a mess," I explained.

"You're not a mess, Ruthie." Randel said with a smile. "No one is perfect."

"I'm not trying to be perfect," I replied.

"Have you considered that rather than you not being the one maybe they were not the one for you?"

"How is that possible when I'm the one

with the issue?"

"Well, and forgive me because I'm about to get biblical with a self-proclaimed heathen," Randel said with a wink and a smile, "but when God sends us the one, all of our so called issues are no longer issues. It is a part of who we are. True love sees perfection in the midst of imperfection."

"So you're saying that I've just been wasting my time because my one hasn't shown up yet?" I asked.

"Basically," he chuckled. "Or maybe you're just not ready to receive him yet. Get to a place where you are happy with you in all your imperfections and leave the rest to God. Then try seeing with your heart."

"In other words, get out my head."

I squeezed Randel's hand and smiled back at him. He'd managed to help me make sense of something that didn't make much sense at all.

"Pastor, I believe you're wanted in the back," a woman with a neon green skirt suit and a large brim hat to match said as she stood two pews ahead of us.

"Oh, um, honey, come here for a moment," Randel stood up and wrapped his arms around the woman's waist as she approached. "Ruth this is my wife, Veronica. Sweetheart, this is Ruth, the one I told you about."

"It's a pleasure to finally meet you, Ruth. Great to put a face to a name," Veronica said with a bright welcoming smile.

"The pleasure is all mine. You guys have a great church," I said not knowing what to say to the woman who was married to the man that I thought I would be married to.

"Sweetheart, can you let them know that I'll be back there in a moment. I just need to say goodbye to Ruth," Randel said to Veronica.

"Of course. It was great to meet you, Ruth. Please visit us again soon," she said.

"Thanks. I will," I said to her.

After Veronica walked off, I walked up close to Randel and said, "You're right. I wouldn't have been a good preacher's wife. I couldn't pull off that hat."

Randel's smile met mine, "You got jokes. I have you know, that's the style in this place."

"More evidence to prove your point," I giggled and gave Randel a hug.

"I really did miss you, Ruth," he whispered in my ear.

"I missed you, too," I responded.

As he let me go, he asked, "Are you

sure you're okay?"

"Yeah, I think I am," I answered.

I left Randel's church and made Mona drop me home without any stops. I went and lied down on my sofa and fell asleep. When I woke up, it was almost dark outside. I walked out to my back patio and stood in the doorway. The night air felt so good as it blew across my face. Then the saxophone began to play. The song was lighter and had a joy to it. I lifted my eyes and saw a slight image of someone sitting in the window with the saxophone to their lips. I tried to look closer but I couldn't see the person's face. Letting go of my curiosity, I sat down and let my heart be filled by the sound.

It had been about a week since I saw Randel and I wasn't sure what I had come away with from the experience. I guess I started to slowly take in what Randel had said, that those guys were not the one for me. So maybe I should stop beating myself up for not being the perfect girlfriend, the one that a man would deem to be the one. Maybe I just needed to go back to focusing on me and let things happen as they should. It was time to stop beating myself up and just let go.

It was early morning and the sun was barely out, but I felt the need to go out for a walk. There was a park not far from my house; Curtis and I used to go there for our daily jogs. It had great scenic views and walking trails. I went there and tried to jog but didn't seem to have the energy. I sat down on a bench that overlooked a small pond and watched as people walked or ran by.

"Ruth," a male voice called out from my right.

I turned my head to see Bo who looked to be out for a morning jog. "Oh hi," I said to him.

He walked up to me and said, "Is everything okay?"

"Yes, sure. I'm fine," I said. "I just needed a little air."

"Oh," he replied. "Do you mind if I sit down?"

"Sure, but aren't you in the middle of a jog?"

"I think I've done enough for the day," he said. "You look like you may need to talk. I know we don't know each other well but I'm all ears."

"You ever feel like your life may need a

makeover but not sure what that makeover should be?" I asked him.

"Yeah, I've been there. But I've found that sometimes it's not a makeover that's needed; we just need to look at our lives through different lenses," he told me.

"I guess," I replied.

"Um, listen, what are you doing tomorrow night?" he asked.

"I don't have anything planned. Why?" I replied.

"There's someplace I'm going and I would really like it if you would come with me. It might help put you in a better headspace," he responded.

"I don't know," I said.

"Why? Because you still think I'm a dude fresh out of prison?" Bo chuckled.

"I didn't, I won't . . . that damn Mona. What else did she tell you?" I said feeling pretty embarrassed.

Bo let out a hardy laugh. "It's okay. But I promise you, you can trust me."

"Okay." I agreed. For some reason, something inside me told me that I could trust Bo. There was something about him; I couldn't put my finger on what it was. His eyes just looked at me differently. As if they've known me for years, as if they were meant to look at me.

"Okay, good. I'll pick you up tomorrow night around seven," he said.

As Bo got up and left, I suddenly started to regret agreeing to go with him. My new goal was to find a way to be at peace with who I am and all of my imperfections. I didn't think I could do that by going on a date with a guy. I wasn't looking to add to my list of exes. My mind was just racing; I was in my head.

The Eyes of Love

Part 7:

He Rested

The Eyes of Love

"So you're going on a date with Bo?" Mona asked as she poured herself another glass of wine.

We sat in Gloria's living room for one of our girls' nights. The topic, of course, was my love life and there was a lot to discuss. I had been on this crazy ride and needed to find the moral of it all. Who better to help me do that than my girls, with the help of a lot of wine?

"It's not a date," I said to her.

"Didn't he ask you?" Mona asked again.

"Yes," I replied.

"And isn't it at night?" she continued.

"Yes," I replied again.

"Then it's a date and I couldn't be happier," Mona said.

"It's not a date," I insisted.

"It kinda sounds like a date to me," Gloria added.

"You too?" I said to Gloria.

"I'm just saying, as dates go, you hit the jackpot," Gloria said.

"How do you know that? You don't even know him?" I asked.

"Who told you that?" she asked. "I have you know we've had some great times with Bo over the past few weeks. He's a really great guy."

"What? When did you guys have great times together and where was I?" I asked.

"You were out with your exes; that's where you were," Gloria said. "Charlie went over one day to Mona's studio to get something and he and Bo really hit it off.

Bo's been over here a few times to do some work in the garage with Charlie."

"There's a lot you don't know about Bo," Mona added.

"I know that you've been telling him all my business," I said to her.

"Oh yeah, there's that. Sorry, but he's really easy to talk to," Mona said. "I think you should give him a chance.

"I think I just need some me time," I said. "Besides, I don't think Bo and I would have anything in common."

"That's interesting because that's the same way you looked at Curtis," Gloria said.

"Don't even," I replied.

"I'm just saying. Go into your date with an open mind and heart; you may be surprised at what you find," Gloria said.

I was tired of listening to my friends, it

was time for me to focus on being okay with me and rushing into a relationship, especially with a guy that I didn't know anything about, was just not the way to do that.

The closer it got to 7 p.m. the more nervous I became. What if Mona and Gloria were right? What if Bo intended for this to be a date? What if he wanted this grand relationship? I was not ready to jump back into the dating pool again. I was not ready to find another guy to add to the ex-boyfriend list. I didn't have the energy to get to know someone or to have someone get to know me. Everything just felt weird for me, like I needed a moment to feel normal again.

I had begun to regret saying yes to Bo. I was pacing up and down my hallway wondering how I could get out of going out with him when the doorbell rang. Bo was standing on the other side looking absolutely gorgeous but the first thing that struck me was the way he looked at me, as if there was nothing more important than me. His eyes lingered on me and he smiled. It was one of those smiles that warmed my whole body and seemed to caress my soul. One of those smiles that made me want to smile back. One of those smiles that made me want to exhale and release all of my doubts.

"You look beautiful," he said.

"Thank you," I blushed.

"Are you ready to go?" he asked.

"Yeah, but where are we going?" I replied.

"You'll see," he gently grabbed hold of my hand and led me to his car.

After driving for a while, we arrived to a part of the art district that almost looked abandoned. Bo pulled up next to a building that looked like an old warehouse but had cars parked alongside it.

"Where are we?" I asked.

"This is Chase's Place," he answered.

"Where?" I asked again.

"It's a lounge that I created in honor of my brother. We have open mic nights where people come and express themselves, however they like. Some through poetry, some through signing, you know, whatever," Bo explained.

"Wow," I proclaimed.

"During the day it serves as a great lunch spot; Grandma Bee does the cooking," he continued.

"That's amazing," I said.

"Come on, let's go in," he instructed.

The inside of Chase's Place was a lot different than the outside. It was almost like walking into someone's comfortable living room. There were the usual table and chairs that you'd find at any night spot but there were also plush sofas with pillows. The lighting was dimed just right and there was an air of familiarity. Everyone seemed to know each other, and they spoke as we walked in.

As we sat on one of the sofas, this guy came up to us; he looked to be a bartender or maybe the manager. He shook Bo's hand and said, "You going on tonight?"

"No, not tonight. I'm just observing," Bo replied.

"So, you actually own this place?" I asked.

"Yeah, I do," he answered.

"And you own the car wash and a construction company?" I continued to ask.

"I do as well," he said.

"Okay, now I'm really curious," I responded.

Bo laughed and turned toward me. "I was a stock broker in New York and did pretty well for myself."

"So what are you doing here?" I asked. "Oh, was it because of what happened to your brother?"

"Yes. When my brother died, it took me a long time to get over it. There was a lot of guilt. I felt like I didn't do enough for him, so I quit my job and moved back home. I started all these businesses to honor him, to make sure his life wasn't in vain," Bo explained.

"Wow, I had you all wrong."

"That's alright. Maybe one day, when you're ready, you'll see me because I'm right here."

"You don't think I see you?"

"I don't know; you tell me."

"I think I do. I may have gotten you wrong in the beginning, but I think I get you now."

"Do you? Or are you looking at me through tinted lenses?"

"I have no clue what you're talking about."

"Well when my brother died, my whole life and everything in it was based on that one moment in time. I hated the world; I didn't trust people and I blamed everyone for my brother not being here."

"I'm sorry that you had to go through that, but I'm not sure how that relates to me."

"Maybe it doesn't; it's just a reminder that we need to let go of things we can't fix and once we do that, we start seeing things through clearer lenses."

I sat back on my chair and turned my head toward the stage. Bo's words were hitting home for me. It was as if he knew exactly what I needed to hear, the way I needed to hear it. I got so caught up in what he was saying that I forgot to make sure he knew we were not on a date. I actually didn't care how our evening together was defined any more.

We spent the rest of the night listening to different people get up on stage and do their thing. There were incredible poets and talented singers. Some people played instruments and one guy even got up and drew a portrait on stage. It was probably one of the best nights I had in a really long time. People were releasing who they are and being comfortable and confident within themselves. They were living their lives in that moment without a care of anything that was weighing them down. They stopped thinking and just started being. I realized I needed to do the same.

After Bo dropped me home, I thanked him for the night. I had begun to see Bo in a whole new light and my friends were right; he was a pretty good guy. The gentle way he would hold me through the night made me feel safe. Every word that came out of his mouth spoke to a piece of me that felt lost, in search for something that made sense in the world. The entire night with Bo felt like I was where I was supposed to be.

I closed the door behind Bo and went to sit outside on my back porch. I was sure my saxophone had a song that fit what I was feeling. But the saxophone didn't play and I sat there for a while waiting to hear. Then softly it started. It sounded like a warm smile that was caressing my soul and eyes that lingered on my body.

I woke up the next morning greeted by the rain. The sound of it was so soothing that I couldn't help but linger in bed a little while longer. I probably would've stayed even longer had Mona not called and completely interrupted my peace.

"So, how was the date?" she asked.

"It wasn't a date," I insisted.

"Okay then, how was the thing that wasn't a date but looked a whole lot like a date?" she asked again sarcastically.

"Funny," I replied, "it actually wasn't

bad. Did you know he was a stock broker in New York?"

"Yeah, he told me," she responded.

"Of course you did. Is there anything else about this man that I should know?" I said.

"Is there anything you would like to know?" she asked sounding like there was a huge smile on her face.

"No," I said.

"If you say so. Don't forget that tonight is the grand reopening of my studio," she said.

"What?" I shouted, almost jumping out of bed. "You're reopening your studio? When did your studio get finished?"

"Oh, I thought I told you," she said as if it was no big deal. "Bo and his crew did a great job. Anyway, I have to go, but see you tonight."

"Wait, what time?" I tried to ask before Mona hung up, but it was too late.

After Mona's call, I lied back down and allowed the sound of the rain to take me back to sleep. When I finally woke up, it was mid-afternoon, and my phone was lit up. I had a missed call from Gloria, who basically wanted to know the same information as Mona, my date with Bo. Then I had a text from Mona telling me what time to be at her grand reopening. But the text that caught my eye was from Bo, asking if I was alright and telling me that he had a good time the night before. I wanted to text or call back, but I didn't know what to do about Bo. He was intriguing to me but so were all the other guys. The timing just seemed off. I needed to figure out my life and not try to fit a guy into it, at least not now.

I could admit that I was wrong about Bo but that didn't mean I should jump into a relationship with him. I think what I learned from all this is that I needed to take care of me first. Maybe someday I'd be ready for a guy like Bo. I put all thoughts out of my head and got out of bed to get dressed.

The rain had stopped a bit as I made my way to Mona's studio for her grand reopening. By the time I got there, the place was already pretty full. There were crowds of people walking around and enjoying all the artwork that was hanging from the walls and displayed on pedestals in the middle of the floor. I had to admit that Bo and his team did a great job; Mona's studio looked beautiful.

I saw Gloria and Charlie standing over to my right and I walked over to greet them.

"Well if it isn't 'miss don't return

calls,'" Gloria said.

"I'm sorry but I knew why you were calling and I just didn't feel like discussing it right then," I explained.

"How about I leave you ladies alone," Charlie said as he gave Gloria a kiss and walked away.

"So, how was the date?" Gloria asked.

"I thought I said I didn't want to talk about it?" I replied.

"You said you didn't want to talk about it then; this is now," Gloria responded with a smile.

I shook my head and said, "I actually had a good time."

"He's a great guy, isn't he?" she said with a huge smile.

"He is," I answered, "but I'm not sure if I'm ready for that, not after what I've just went through."

"Ruth, have you considered that what you discovered about your past and your exes and yourself, was all to prepare you for a guy like Bo?" Gloria asked.

"I don't know . . ." I said but stopped mid-sentence. I hadn't considered it. The truth was I didn't know what everything meant. I knew there was something that I was supposed to learn from all this, but I'm not sure I was clear on what that thing was.

I guess my take away from these last few months is that I couldn't be everything to everyone. There's no way to be the perfect woman to every guy. So, until that guy comes along who I can be perfect for, I'll continue to be my best self living my life in a way that makes me happy.

"Ruth, everything is going to be alright. Just trust that, okay?" Gloria held my hand and gave me a wink. "Speaking of everything being alright, Bo's over there. If you're not going to pursue him, maybe you should let him know that."

Gloria was right. I had to say something to Bo, explain to him about this weird place that I was in. Hopefully, he'd understand and not think I wasn't interested or blowing him off.

I walked over to Bo who had his back to me and said hi. He turned around to face me with a smile and said hi back. The look on Bo's face was welcoming. His smile was comforting. It almost made me lose my breath.

"I'm sorry I didn't call you back," I said.

"That's alright. I figured we would meet up sooner or later," he replied with a grin.

"I had a good time last night," I said.

"So did I. Hopefully, we can do it

again," he responded.

"Um, I don't know. It's not that I don't want to I just, I don't know. I'm in a weird place right now . . ." I tried to tell him.

Bo stopped me and said, "Sometimes the best things happen to us while we're in weird places."

"Did you read that someplace?" I asked with a smile.

"No, just some life lessons," he said. "Listen, I'm not asking for anything from you, only what you're comfortable with." Bo turned to walk off but stopped and turned back to me saying, "Maybe one day it'll all make sense."

Bo gave me one final smile and walked away. Mona and Gloria must have been somewhere close by watching and listening because they walked over as soon as Bo had left.

"Are you seriously just going to let him get away?" Mona asked.

"What do you want me to do?" I replied.

"Go after him," Mona said.

"Ruth, this man has lived through pain; he's healed and used that pain to be a blessing to so many young people. Is that really the kind of guy you want to let walk out of your life?" Gloria explained.

"I know he's a great guy, but it's just . . . do you know that the best relationship that I have had in a really long time is with a saxophone?" I said to them.

"I'm sorry, what?" Mona looked at me as if I had lost my mind.

"I know it sounds weird. But I got a new neighbor a few months back and whoever they are, they play the saxophone and that saxophone greets me every night.

It consoles me when I cry and keeps me company when I'm lonely. It's like that saxophone knows my every need. I find myself rushing home just to hear that saxophone. I realized that's what and who Mr. Right is; he just knows me without me speaking and accepts every aspect of who I am," I explained.

"That's absolutely beautiful, Ruth. As much as I thought Mona's idea was ridiculous, I think it really did you some good," Gloria said giving me a hug.

"I didn't realize a saxophone could do all that. Maybe I should call that musician I met the other day. Do you think drums would have the same effect?" Mona looked back and forth between Gloria and me waiting for a response, but we didn't give her one.

Gloria just shook her head and turned to

me asking, "So, what are you going to do, Ruth?"

"I'm going to go home and spend time with my saxophone," I replied with a smile.

By the time I got home, the rain had started again. It increasingly got worse to the point where it was thundering and my lights were flickering. I changed into some sweats and cuddled up on my sofa. Everything was quiet and I began to wonder what happened to my saxophone. I walked over to my kitchen and opened my back door. The lights seemed to be off and no one appeared to be home.

I sat on my swing and sipped my wine. I wanted to wait for my saxophone because it was all I had, and the crazy part is that I was alright with that. The wind began to pick up and a large thunder roared through the skies. I got up to go back inside but the moment I turned to walk in, the saxophone began to play. I stopped mid step and smiled. I stood there for a moment enjoying the sound. It was as if the hand of love was rubbing my shoulders and massaging my neck; it felt fantastic.

I turned around slowly and let the wind beat against my face, as the saxophone kissed my lips. My head was clear and my heart was enjoying the beauty of the moment. A couple of drops of rain landed on my face and as I wiped it off, I looked up and saw him.

"Oh my God!" I yelled out and ran back into my house grabbing my rain boots that sat next to the door.

I opened my front door and ran outside,

leaving behind my coat and umbrella. I ran over to the house next door and started pounding on the door. I couldn't believe what I was doing but I had to get inside that house; I had to get to him.

"I know it's you. Open the door!" I shouted.

The door opened and there was Bo, holding the saxophone. He smiled and said, "You could have just rung the bell."

"It was you?" I asked.

"You're soaked, come in," he said leading me into his house.

He went into his bathroom and came back out with a big towel to wrap around me. The whole time he was drying me off, I couldn't keep my eyes off him. It was like I was seeing him for the first time and my heart began to fill up.

"Why did you, did you know . . .?" I

tried to ask all the questions that were trying to form in my head but the words couldn't come out.

"Come with me," Bo said as he took hold of my hand and led me up the stairs.

We came to a room that looked like an office but had pictures on the wall and a chair next to the window. By the chair was a saxophone stand.

Bo pointed to the window and said, "Look through the window and tell me what you see."

I walked over to the window and saw my backyard, my swing that sat on my back porch and my back window showing into my kitchen.

"So you've been watching me?" I asked.

"Not in a creepy way. When I first moved in, I came up here to do some work in my office and I saw you sitting on your porch. At first, I was just practicing. I thought at some point you would come over and yell at me to stop. But you didn't; you seemed to enjoy it, so I kept playing. Then you walked into my car wash and I got a closer look, and you are absolutely beautiful, Ruth," he explained.

After a slight pause with him staring into my eyes, he continued. "Anyway, after that you just looked like you could use some company or an escape, so I played songs for you, something to help you feel better. I hope it did."

"It did actually," I said. "But why didn't you say anything?"

"I don't know. I wanted to. But it never seemed like the right time; you always seemed distracted, like there were more important things going on," he answered.

"Yeah, stuff that I thought was important."

"Ruth, I think you are absolutely perfect and would just like the chance to show you how great we would be."

"You think I'm perfect? I mean, you didn't notice how slightly neurotic I can be?

"Yeah, I noticed that," he smiled at me and softly caressed my face.

His hands felt like they were made to touch me. I looked at Bo and my heart saw him. I saw everything in him that I had been looking for. I saw a man who cared enough about me to console me, even from a distance, and respected me enough to give me the space I needed to find out who I was. I saw a man who, even though I misjudged him, refused to let me go and always seemed to always be around when I needed him. I saw a man who saw my perfection in my imperfections. I saw him, and he looked like love.

Bo & Ruth

"Then she said, sit still, my daughter, until you know how the matter will fall: for the man will not be in rest..."

Ruth 3:18

Epilogue

The sunlight pierced through the blinds and landed on my eyelids. I slowly opened my eyes and it landed on Bo's sleeping face. I wanted to touch him, to make sure he was real, something I'd caught myself doing every morning for the past six months.

I couldn't believe he was real. That I loved this man and that I was being loved by this man. I had never felt so free, so much like myself. I could finally be me, and for the first time I felt like someone had all of me and I had all of them. My soul was at peace in his hands. I smiled to myself, as I realized how fortunate I was that he had found me.

"Why are you smiling?" Bo asked as he opened his eyes and stared at me.

"Just thinking," I replied.

"About what?" he asked again.

"About you. About how happy I am that you're here," I answered with a content grin.

"Well, get used to being happy because I don't plan on going anywhere," Bo replied.

As we leaned in to kiss, the phone rang. I whined out loud, "Oh no." I leaned over and grabbed the phone. Before I could say hello, a voice yelled out on the other end, "Ruth, you better come get this old lady out my kitchen!"

"Mona? What old lady?" I asked.

"Grandma Bee! She keeps calling me a fast tail heffa," Mona explained.

"Why is Grandma Bee in your kitchen?" I asked.

"Well, technically it's Gloria's kitchen, but I don't see the difference since I'm here," she replied.

"Okay, calm down. I'm on my way," I said.

"Good. But you better hurry up, otherwise you'll be scraping old lady from the ceiling," Mona warned before hanging up the phone.

I held my head in my hand and started to laugh. Grandma Bee and Mona were like oil and water ever since they first met; I sometimes regret ever introducing them. But their bickering amused me, mostly because Grandma Bee was always pretty dead on with her words to Mona and Mona hated that.

"Don't tell me they're already fighting?" Bo asked.

"Yes they are," I said with a chuckle. "I better get over there."

"Okay. I need to get over to the car wash anyway," Bo said as he leaned over and kissed me.

"See you later?" I asked.

"Absolutely," he replied.

My day was pretty full. Gloria and Charlie were having a dinner party for family and friends and I agreed to help out. But I would've dropped all of that just to stay in Bo's arms.

I quickly showered and dressed and made my way over to Gloria's house. When I got there, Mona was in full hysteria and

Grandma Bee was looking at her with that stern motherly glare. Gloria was standing between them trying desperately to hold back her laughter.

"Ruth!" Gloria yelled out when she saw me walk in. "I'm so glad you're here.

"Hi. Is everything alright?" I asked.

"I told you about her," Mona said.

Grandma Bee turned to me and softly smiled saying, "Don't pay any attention to that crazy child. Hi baby. Are you hungry?"

She gave me the warmest hug and then left to go into the kitchen, convinced that I needed something to eat.

"That old lady hates me," Mona said when Grandma Bee left the room.

"No she doesn't," I replied.

"I think she actually does," Gloria said with a giggle.

"Maybe just try being nice to her and

not argue back," I told Mona.

"That won't help. She keeps telling me that I'm never going to get a man with my bad attitude," Mona said.

"Well . . ." Gloria started to say.

"Well nothing!" Mona yelled out. "I don't have a bad attitude and I do have a man."

"Who?" Gloria and I asked in unison.

"Donald." Mona responded.

"Donald who?" I continued to ask.

"The accountant," she answered.

"Wait, Donald the accountant who's allergic to the world?" I asked again.

"Yes, that Donald. Gloria referred him to help get my finances together at my studio and we hit it off. Besides, you guys know I like a project," Mona explained.

Gloria and I erupted in laughter, knowing full well that poor Donald didn't stand a chance with Mona.

"Just let her have that one," Gloria said, shaking her head.

Grandma Bee yelled at us from the kitchen, insisting that we stop chit chatting and get our butts in there. We moved without hesitation, fearing the wrath of Grandma Bee. We joined Grandma Bee in the kitchen and began preparing the food for Gloria's dinner party. Meanwhile, Charlie was in the backyard with a few of the boys from Bo's car wash setting up. I thought it was such a great idea to have the dinner party outside. After all, it was a beautiful spring day and could only be an even more beautiful night.

When we were done preparing the food, Gloria let Grandma Bee take a nap in her guest room. I looked at my watch and realized that I didn't have much time to go home and get ready. I went to grab my purse so that I could quickly make it home and back in time.

"Where are you going?" Gloria asked me.

"Home, to get dressed." I replied.

"No need. There's something here for you to wear," she said.

"Yeah, I picked it out," Mona added with excitement.

"I don't really feel like being half naked tonight," I said, knowing Mona's style.

"Hey, the dress is cute. It's sexy and classy," Mona said.

"It is a cute dress, Ruth. I made sure she didn't go overboard," Gloria said with a smile.

"I wish you guys told me we were getting dressed here. I would have brought all my things over," I told them feeling confused as to why we needed to get dressed together.

"Don't worry; we'll take care of all of that," Gloria said as she and Mona led me upstairs and into Gloria's bedroom.

There was a beautiful blue dress that laid across the bed. Seeing it immediately put a smile on my face. Blue was Bo's favorite color and he would always say that it's his favorite color because of how beautiful it looked on me.

The three of us spent a few hours upstairs talking, laughing and getting ready for the evening. Before long it had gotten dark outside and Grandma Bee came into the room telling us to hurry up. Then she looked over to me and smiled with her eyes.

"You look absolutely beautiful sweetheart," Grandma Bee said to me.

"Thank you," I replied smiling back at

her.

"The only thing is your makeup is a bit much," Grandma Bee added.

"Hey, I did her makeup," Mona proclaimed.

"That explains it," Grandma Bee said under her breath.

Mona waived her fist in the air as Grandma Bee walked past her to pick up a tissue from the table. I mouthed over to her, "Be nice."

Grandma Bee came over to me and began to wipe off some of the makeup from my face. She then held my face in her hand and said, "There. Now you look gorgeous as always." She then looked at Mona with one eye and continued, "See, that's how you're supposed to wear makeup."

Mona began to wave her finger at Grandma Bee now about to explode. Gloria grabbed her and started pushing her out the room.

"Alright, how about we all head downstairs," Gloria said.

Something seemed off as we approached the bottom of the stairs. Everything was calm and quiet. Mona, Gloria and Grandma Bee all had weird expressions on their faces; it was a mixture between pure joy and anticipation.

When we arrived to the back door, there were two of the boys from Bo's car wash standing in front of the closed door dressed in tuxedos. I suspiciously smiled at them, asking them what they were doing there. But they only smiled gleefully at me. Then they opened the door and Gloria pushed me in front of them. When I walked into the backyard, my mouth dropped. It was eloquently lit with small decorative candles and filled long stem red roses.

I turned to Gloria who had been joined by Charlie and started to say, "It's beaut . . ." But the sound of my saxophone playing cut my words short. I turned and there was Bo, playing for me once again. I could hear every sentence, every word, every syllable. I covered my mouth with my quivering hands and tears of joy fell down my cheeks. When he was done, I nodded my head yes continuously and ran and jumped into his arms.

"I'm lost. What just happened? Is that it?" Mona asked.

"Hush," Grandma Bee instructed her.

Bo placed both my feet back on the ground. Then he got on one knee and took out the most incredible ring I had ever seen and placed it on my finger. The tears couldn't stop running down my face. I kissed Bo, knowing that he was mine forever.

Everyone ran up to us and began hugging us and clapping. Then Mona stood back and asked, "Okay, what the hell did that saxophone say to you that obviously the rest of us didn't hear."

I looked into the eyes of my love and replied, "It said that I was the one."

www.ingramcontent.com/pod-product-compliance
Lightning Source LLC
Chambersburg PA
CBHW031944130726
47905CB00002BA/538